Black Butterflies

Sara Alexi is the author of the Greek Village Series.
She divides her time between England and a small village
in Greece.

http://facebook.com/authorsaraalexi

Sara Alexi

BLACK BUTTERFLIES

oneiro

Published by Oneiro Press 2012

Copyright © Sara Alexi 2012

This edition 2015

ISBN - 1479399531
ISBN 13 - 9781479399536

Chapter 1

Across the water the island looks harmless. From this distance it is a misty blue, undefined, drifting above the horizon. The sun shines without a care, lazy, hot. No sounds are heard except the lap of the water and the snuffle of a stray dog.

'You are coming, lady? Time to go,' the man says, rope in hand. The brown, sleek-coated dog sniffs around his polished shoes. He flicks the end of the rope at it and the mongrel sidesteps and turns its attention to the woman on the bench.

Marina refocuses her eyes on the young man. The island fades behind him.

'Sorry?' She slips her arm through the handle of her old leather bag, anticipating his reply.

'Let's go.' He nods his head at the boat, which he has hold of with one hand, one foot on board, one on the shore, the strength of his inner thighs keeping it from drifting. He releases the mooring line from the quay's solitary rusting iron bollard in readiness to be under way.

Planting her feet firmly, shoulder width apart, Marina leans her upper body weight forward over her shins, her black skirt taut in the effort as she slowly straightens. Her back isn't so bad at the moment. Perhaps she needs to lose a kilo or two, but all day long in her corner shop with sweets, crisps, biscuits, and often there seems little point in cooking for one...

Her black bag, hooked in the crook of her elbow, slides from the bench as she straightens, the weight jerking her slightly to one side.

She is glad she has not worn her new shoes. The concrete pier is pitted and crumbling. She struggles to reach across the sea-filled gap for the handrail and the captain helps by taking the bag, slipping it up his own arm and steadying her descent into the small craft. It lurches with her weight and rocks as it stabilises.

It has been a long time since Marina has been on one of these boats. She blinks back a silent tear, recalling the last time she was forced to make this journey, all those years ago. Inside the boat, the cushioned box seats and the plastic windows in the plywood cabin walls are a thin veneer of civilisation; despite these additions it is still a basic wooden fishing boat, layers of paint a testament to its long service.

In the prow of the boat facing the sea-etched windows and the tiny ship's wheel is a big leather bucket seat on a thick chrome stanchion. The captain trots down the steps into the vessel and grabs the back of this perch and eases himself into it, demonstrating not only that it can rotate but also that it has an internal shock absorber and is quite happy to bob up and down once loaded with the weight of a man. Marina's mirth escapes as an audible giggle and he grins back at her, raising an eyebrow.

'Hot today,' he remarks.

Marina nods.

Settling into his throne, he carefully arranges his coffee mug, cigarettes and lighter around him. Marina, giggles forgotten, is suddenly aware that she is at the point of no return. Memories flood her thoughts and she swallows hard, deciding that perhaps the journey is not such a good idea after all. She takes hold of her bag and, planting her feet on the floor, eases her weight forward. Unaware, the captain flicks a switch and the revving engine rocks Marina back into her seat, the deep throb of diesel drowning out her half-hearted protests. His attention is now on the sea. Edging the throttle forward, he swings his taxi boat away from the pier, leaving Marina to come to terms with the decision she has not quite made. She looks out at the blue.

Even though the sea is flat-calm and silky smooth, once some speed has been gained the hull begins an irregular bounce against the water, booming in the plywood cabin. The spray from the bow blows in through the open doorways spasmodically, like indecisive rain. The man sits on his pedestal, bouncing to its rhythm, throttle fully forward. He leans to his right and flicks another switch on a small home-made plywood box. The craft fills with the sounds of eighties pop music and the captain sings along, the words distorted by his thick accent. His brown polished shoes tap out the rhythm on the worn wooden floor. Marina cannot help but think more practical shoes would be better suited to the job. But his open-necked shirt is clean and his jeans have an ironed crease down the centre. It is nice to see a well turned out young man.

Her attention is drawn back to the island, but as it does not seem to be getting any bigger Marina pushes thoughts of it away and turns to look back towards the mainland, beyond the boat's wake, which rises and curls upon itself. Plumes of spray create rainbows. Beyond, the mainland is receding. The dog is still on the pier, sniffing around the bench where she sat. The shore on either side of the pier is rough and pebbly. There are no tourists there; it is just a port, a place of comings and goings. Not much has changed, the farmhouse just as she remembers it from all that time ago. There are more cars parked now than when she was a girl. But there were fewer people everywhere in those days. Everyone knew everyone back then. That was why Aunt Efi took her to the island. Marina crosses herself three times and blesses the memory of Aunt Efi, and then curses her in the same breath, blinking back more unexpected tears. It is silly after all these years.

A new song bubbles from the speakers. The captain is whistling along to the music and his chair bounces in rhythm as his foot pushes the beat into the floor. Some wisps of his hair are blowing in the wind that curls through the two forward doors. He becomes aware of Marina's stare and raises a hand to slick back the stray strands, but no sooner has he smoothed his mane than the wind regains its wild control. The captain pauses his singing and grooming to light a cigarette. He catches Marina's eye as he turns from the wind to still the lighter flame and smiles cheerfully, nodding to the island to indicate their advance.

Marina can see the town now. The long streak of an island is broken in the middle by what looks, from this distance, more like a tumble of white rocks. She can make out a vague indentation, indicating the harbour opening. She puts a hand to her stomach and wishes she had eaten more for breakfast, or less. The island seemed bigger all those years ago, but her nerves felt the same.

The land is now fast approaching, the houses cascading down to the port from the pine trees on the ridge. Red-tiled roofs atop dazzling whitewashed walls. Small, contained, as ancient as Greece itself.

They are approaching with speed. Now she can clearly see the high stone wall to the left of the port entrance, capped with dots of black, a line of old cannons. She looks to the right to make out the lower wall, also sporting rusted cannons to complete the defence. She watched a documentary about the island on television one night when business was quiet in the shop. It was a wealthy port, full of merchants, shipping magnates, at one time. Pirates were a constant threat, so the islanders slung a chain across the harbour entrance, from cannon to cannon. The heavy chain dipped beneath the waves to catch on the keels of the invading boats, giving the islanders time to load and fire at will.

Marina half wishes the chain were in place now so that their keel might be caught, ensuring their return to the mainland. She could hop on the first bus back to the village and the shop, with familiar faces coming and going, and routines that seldom vary, with childhood friends who became parents, who now come in with their grandchildren. Time standing still, until you look in the mirror.

The captain is singing Queen's 'Fat Bottomed Girls' at the top of his voice. He has slid from his elevation and is all but dancing as he steers. He lets go of the wheel for a full spin before slicking his hair back and continuing towards the port.

Marina laughs, her eyes sparkling. The man turns to smile at her and offers his hand for a dance. She waves him away. He grins.

Voices, an American twang, can be heard, and Marina looks about her through the salt-streaked plastic windows. There is a sailing yacht also heading for the port, the crew on deck in bright swimwear, with pasty white limbs. They wave and laugh and the captain sounds his horn in one loud, rude blast, and he sings all the louder. The day trippers laugh and wave more vigorously. The captain smooths his hair, sticks out his chest.

The cannons are nearly above them now. They have reached the entrance to the harbour. The captain shuts down the engine and their speed drops to a lulling chug. The bouncing becomes wallowing, everything calm. Only Marina's stomach churns. She reminds herself that she is here for a purpose, a mission that takes priority over her own comfort.

The once peaceful harbour has changed almost beyond recognition and she is surprised by the mayhem, the shouts, the tangled anchors and the cluster of vessels, some of them huge. Million-dollar yachts tied to the quay next to tiny speedboats, chartered sailing yachts next to private gin palaces. The harbour is heaving. The early birds have moored themselves in stern first, up against the port wall; the latecomers are bow first, nuzzling in between those that are safely harboured, adding a line where they can, tying one to another, three vessels deep in some places. There is scarcely any room left to manoeuvre in the middle of the port.

With the engine idling, Marina can hear some Athenians on their day-sailing yacht asking permission to cross an expensive-looking schooner, to make their way to shore. There is no response to their Greek request, and they speak again in strongly accented English. The Asian in uniform on the schooner waves them across, the sea their joint pleasure, and mutual fear, levelling all social boundaries. The sound of these calls, Marina decides, is a happy one, and she smiles, pushing her own fear to one side.

It is just possible for Marina to see the island's fishing boats, tiny traditional wooden vessels, double-ended, tightly squeezed into a corner. An arch through the high pier gives them access to the sea, allowing them to bypass the hordes of pleasure boats.

Marina and her captain have all but stopped, and he is manoeuvring them carefully alongside the area reserved for taxi boats and the commercial hydrofoils, the 'Flying Dolphins'. Once lined up, he jumps onto land and makes fast to an iron ring set into the stone quayside before descending to help Marina with her bag. Marina hesitates and struggles to gain her balance. She toys with the idea of paying double and returning immediately, but knows she must go ashore.

'Next time, I will play only Greek music and we will stop halfway across and dance,' the captain laughs.

Marina hauls herself ashore and rummages in her big bag to find a smaller bag, from which she takes her purse.

'You will do no such thing!' She pays him, with a grin.

'When we are halfway across, who will stop us?'

Marina giggles and the years drop away, their age difference suspended. The man smiles and jumps back aboard his boat to answer a call on the radio. Seat bobbing, he revs the engine and is away with a wink and a wave.

Marina puts her purse away, takes a deep breath and looks up, her smile fading. The town is all still there, just as it was then. The stumpy clock tower, the impressive Venetian mansions. She tries to calm her thoughts by recalling what the documentary said, about the shipowners bringing such wealth to the island, but the facts won't be recalled. The port has changed in some respects since her last visit. The wide walkway around the port is now a mass of cafés, with chairs and tables up to the water's edge. Where she is standing is very busy, every chair taken, the spaces between full of suitcases, as people, yawning at this early hour, wait to move on.

'Marina?'

Marina turns to the sea of people, a habitual smile of response brightening her face.

'Marina, over here!'

Marina sees a woman, waving, who looks vaguely familiar.

'Marina, do you remember me?'

'Hello!' Marina smiles as she recalls the woman's face; she came into the shop in the village one day, a while ago, not this summer anyway. Now, what did she buy? Ah yes! Two bottles of wine (in glass, mind you, not the local stuff in plastic bottles), bread and eggs, before declaring that she and her husband were lost. They stayed for ages chatting, her husband interpreting. Wasn't this the American couple? She brought in chairs from the back to make them more comfortable. Lovely people. Yes, they chatted so long that when they left she forgot to ask them to pay. He was called Bill – Vasillis in Greek… but what was her name?

'I cannot believe you are here! I mean, what are the odds? Do you know, we were trying to work out if we could pass by your shop this time around, but I am not sure we even remember where it is. We felt so bad. Did you realise we forgot to pay?' She looks expectantly at Marina.

'No speak English.' Marina is glad of a lifetime of American films and the occasional tourist in the shop. She understands English fairly well but she struggles to speak it. She uses her lack of fluency to avoid embarrassing the woman over the money. A man approaches from inside the café, wiping his hands on his white shorts.

'Bill, look who I've found.'

'Come on, dear, the boat is coming. Oh – Marina!' He continues clumsily in Greek. 'How fortuitous. Do you know we left without paying you? We've felt terrible.' He scrabbles in his money belt and hands Marina a note. It is far more than they owe. Marina waves it away, but the man insists and tucks it into her bag. 'What on earth are you doing here? I thought you never left your little village? '

'I feel almost as if we have willed you here.' The woman laughs. Marina is not surprised at the meeting. She knows Greece brings you the people you search for, be it for friendship, business, love, or just to pay for a bottle of wine.

She opens her mouth to speak, but Bill continues. 'I was going to send you the money, but all I knew was you kept a shop in a village! So it was never going to get to you. I can't believe–' He is interrupted as the people all around them spark into life, and he looks around to see what the cause is. The Flying Dolphin is rounding the harbour wall. Suitcases are heaved. Chatter grows. Money is waved at the waiter, who shows no sign of hurry. His agility and grace through the crowds of people and their belongings is only surpassed by the litheness of the stray cats slinking through the forest of feet. The woman (*what is her name?*) carries on regardless.

'I feel so much better now we're straight. How are you? Did your daughter's wedding go all right?' she asks.

'Yes, good.' Marina's eyes light up at the memory.

'Your youngest, wasn't it? No, don't tell me, it's good for me to try to remember things. Eleni!'

Marina laughs and shakes her head, and opens her mouth to speak.

'No, no! Eleni's your eldest. Just a minute… Artemis! How could I forget such a pretty name! Any children yet?'

Marina shakes her head sadly.

'Darling, the boat's going to leave. Come on.'

'Bill! Will you take a photo of Marina and me? I cannot believe we have met up again. So lovely to see you.'

'Darling, there really isn't time.'

'Oh, come on, Bill. They haven't even tied up yet. The people haven't even got off, and there's a huge queue to get on. We have loads of time.' The lady begins to search through her rucksack.

Marina looks over to the hydrofoil. It is pulling alongside the quay. There is a girl on board throwing a rope to a man on the shore. She wears a black uniform, a peaked hat and inappropriately high

13

heels. Marina tuts. She finds it hard to imagine her elder daughter, Eleni, doing the same job. She was so young when she took herself off to Piraeus to join up. Marina's head shakes sadly. The high heels click on the gangplank. Surely she cannot be port police? Maybe the uniform is similar and this woman works on the Flying Dolphin – Marina is not sure. 'Come here, next to me, Marina. So what are you doing here? Take it with the café in the background, Bill. Oh yes, didn't you say your eldest daughter was coming to work here? Smile. Thanks, Bill.'

'Come on, dear, we really must make a move.' Bill stuffs the camera into a bag around his waist. 'Marina, it has been a delightful surprise. I wish you all the best.'

'I loved your shop, Marina. We have such good memories of that holiday. What with all your goat bells and shepherd's crooks and fresh bread, and those amazing village eggs, so fresh – it was a regular cornucopia. I wish there was such a well-stocked store near where I live. You must come to the States one day.'

'Darling…'

'Well, goodbye, Marina. Can't imagine why you would want to be here, when your village is so perfect and unspoilt by tourism. This is all a bit much, isn't it? All the best.'

The noise of people embarking and disembarking reaches a clamorous pitch and the woman has to raise her voice. Marina smiles. The girl in the black uniform takes the Americans' tickets, tears them in half, and the two of them disappear into the shadows of the boat, leaving Marina alone.

The growl of the engine as the hydrofoil reverses its way out of the port brings the noise to a climax. It swings through the harbour entrance and disappears round the corner. The din subsides and a peace returns. The cafés are all but empty now, and the waiters loosen their gait in the comparative calm. They chat to each other from their territories about the football last night, the new mayor, what they will do this evening after work. Marina picks up her bag and wonders what to do now she is here. She knows why she has come, but how to go about it?

The harbour is roughly three sides of a square, with a jutting-out pier all but closing the fourth, seaward, side. The harbour is not very large and the really big boats are obliged to moor on the outside in the deeper water – or so the documentary said. Marina feels quite the expert. There are no boats there now. She walks slowly up to the first corner where the donkeys wait to take bags and tourists, furniture and water bottles, anything that needs transporting with more than a handcart. There are no roads here, no cars or motorbikes, only travellers on foot and donkeys on little cobbled lanes: unspoilt, lost in time, a slower pace of life, even for Marina. She sighs with pleasure at the thought of slowing down.

'Hello, lady – you want a donkey to take you and your bag to your hotel? It's either donkey or legs –

there is no other transport here, you know?' His weather-worn face speaks of years in the sun.

'Yes, I know.' Marina remembers trying to stroke the donkeys the last time she was here, and Aunt Efi hurrying her to keep walking. She doesn't suppose it could be the same donkey. 'How old is he?'

'She's about fourteen by now. Come on, I will–'

Marina's attention is caught by another, younger, donkey man. A Japanese girl is being helped up onto the last donkey in the line, and once she is uncomfortably aloft the donkey man lashes her bags to the lead mule. He stops his movements every now and again to twist his handlebar moustache. Neither the moustache, nor the action of twisting it, seems to suit his young age. A Japanese man is circling around them taking photographs, tripping over the cats sprawled on the cool marble flags.

'Who is that?' Marina asks.

'Yanni, but his donkeys are no better than mine, we–'

'How old is he?'

'How old is he? First the donkey, now the man. Well, let me see. He was at school with my son, not the same year, though – the year above, I think, so that will make him thirty-five. Although anybody would be forgiven for thinking he is older. No humour, that one. Old for his age. Not like my boy, so full of life...'

'You say he was at school with your son. So he has been here all his life then?' Marina tries to sound casual.

'He lives with his parents up on the ridge there.' The man points above the houses to the skyline. 'Hey, Yanni, there's a lady asking after you here!'

'Hush up, I was just curious.' Marina smiles and feels her cheeks colour.

Yanni, with the girl and her bags ready, leads them off, holding the first animal's bridle. He glances at Marina before looking away again, without any smile, any pleasantry.

'Good day,' Marina calls, but Yanni just hurries his animals on with the command *'Dai'*, and the procession ambles away, the Japanese man still photographing the spectacle and laughing as he chatters to the girl, who is hanging on with both hands, looking very nervous.

'You won't get much out of Yanni. Now, which hotel am I taking you to?'

'No, no, thank you.' Marina smiles as if to ask his forgiveness as she walks quietly away until she is under the clock tower. She has no hotel booked, she doesn't know where she is going. In fact, it seems ridiculous to be here now. She is not normally one to interfere but the situation is extreme and, as she is the only one who knows, who else can keep Eleni safe? She looks around at the houses encircling the port like an amphitheatre.

The houses highest up, Marina knows, follow the line of a gully which is hidden from view and extend all the way beyond a rocky outcrop to a second tiny harbour a couple of kilometres from the main port to the west.

The only destination she knows is the house she stayed in with Aunt Efi on the other side of this hill. The shallow steps up past the bakery could take her directly there, or she could walk right around the harbour and go along the coast and then inland up that gully, in no hurry. She looks behind her. The donkey man is watching her so she sets off with purpose towards the coastal path; it's as good a direction as any.

Chapter 2

At the far end of the harbour the shops dwindle, and Marina turns the corner along the coastal walk past a jumble of jagged rocks. The port felt so busy and she is glad to be back on her own. She takes a deep breath and exhales the rush.

The sea sparkles, and the rocks drop away and flatten off to the water's edge on her right, where a set of concrete steps has been laid to give access to the sea for bathing. By the steps, she remembers, there is a cave, with waves crashing inside, booming even on a calm day. She recalls young men jumping, laughing, through the hole in the cave's roof to the darkened sea below, climbing out again and prancing their way back up on the sharp, sun-baked rocks, to somersault from the edge of the cave's roof into the deeper water. She longed to join them, and smiled at one of them, but when Aunt Efi pulled her scarf forward to cover her face and marched her onward, the knot in her stomach tightened, the fear increased.

New, painted signs forbid diving and jumping from the cave, but even so there are boys, now in knee-length shorts, ignoring the warnings, laughing, daring each other. She can hear Greek, English, French and German. Back then, it was only Greek. She presses her lips together but her chin quivers.

Marina looks up at the view across the sea, across the narrow strip of water separating the island from the mainland, dotted with islets. They float on white skirts, mingling with the sky. The view is a dreamy series of blues, each island a lighter shade, until in the distance they merge with the sky altogether, neither land nor cloud. Back then, she thought it was the best view she had ever seen. Today it still catches in her throat, swells her chest; she's glad she came for the view alone.

Further up the path is another place she remembers, a sheer rocky cliff – in her mind's eye she once again sees the two men daring each other to jump from higher and higher up. With her heart in her mouth she felt sure they would hit the rocks below, or that they would plunge too deep. But again and again they reappeared, flicking back wet fringes, and laughing. Aunt Efi pulled at her sleeve but Marina dawdled until a few harsh words brought colour to her cheeks and made her bow her head as they walked on.

Today the rock stands bare, and she hears snatches of a foreign conversation, French perhaps, drifting up from the heads bobbing in the water far below. No one is jumping from the rocks. A concrete platform has been built at the bottom, with iron steps into the sea.

The stone-cobbled path continues unchanged until she comes to where the steps drop to a smaller harbour away from the main town. Here, before the descent to where the fishing boats are moored, is a freshly painted taverna. That is new. The most popular restaurant used to be down by the fishing boats, but as Marina descends she sees that the building is now derelict, its windows black, lifeless, the doors nailed shut, faded signs still hanging. It's a sad sight.

The path leads inland, under twisted old pine trees that line the dry riverbed here, past dry wells, now used as dustbins, and onto the wide, gently sloping walkway that leads to the house she once knew. The houses here vary. Small whitewashed shepherds' cottages sit beside large cut-stone mansions – the island's history preserved in rich foreigners' holiday homes. Passing some of the larger houses, she steps closer to look up through the windows. The ceilings in the grander houses have intricate wooden latticework decoration that astonished her as a child. She stares up through a high window. It impresses again today.

A meow draws her attention, and she looks down at a black-and-white cat, just past kittenhood, lithe and muscular. She leans down to stroke its head and the cat raises itself on its back legs to meet her hand. As she walks on, it trots by her ankles. Her old shoes are comfortable on the warm, smooth stones. Marina watches her feet and wonders why her ankles are always so swollen. She's been on her feet for nearly twenty years in her shop, trying to make ends meet as a widow and a single mother. Maybe that's it.

Maybe her ankles need a rest? She sits on a low wall by the path. The cat jumps up next to her. She strokes it.

'Maybe Eleni would not have felt this need to rebel. Maybe she would have stayed at home if she'd had a calmer childhood, a better baba?' Marina addresses the cat. Eleni was eight and little Artemis only three when Manolis was killed. Marina can still recall doing the maths. The orange groves were not really enough without an extra income. It was a sad time, but Marina found she could not grieve for Manolis; he had been too unpredictable, too wild, too selfish. She wouldn't miss him, and he was hardly ever there anyway. But there was a change, and in that change she needed an extra income.

She recalls the day after his death, wandering around their house, coming to terms with the fact that it was now all hers…

Thinking of it as her own put butterflies in her stomach; she felt she was doing something naughty, that Manolis would rise from the grave and shout at her, or ridicule her. She poked a finger into the back of his chair – it was always in the way there. Without premeditation, she grabbed it by the arms and dragged it, grating its wooden feet on the stone flags. When she stood back to consider it in its new position, she felt as if she had slapped Manolis across the face. He liked things to be where they were, no change, even if it made Marina's life more difficult with the children or the cleaning. She continued her wanderings through to the kitchen, and then back. The chair's position felt uncomfortable, and she returned it to its original spot. Eleni, who had come into the kitchen behind her, watched her replace the chair. Silent, her big eyes following Marina's movements, looking just a little too much like Manolis.

After a couple of days it grew easier, with the funeral done and the mourners gone. Her mother left her alone a little more, still taking the dry-eyed grandchildren to amuse them, but allowing Marina a little more space.

Wandering through the house, she tripped on the rug, again, for the hundredth time, and she bent to straighten its edge. It was the ugly, cheap rug he had got from the gypsy. Marina sighed at the memory of those poor gypsies. She remembered, too, Eleni's confusion as she witnessed the event, trying to weigh up right from wrong, and she remembered struggling to find a way to explain her baba's behaviour to the little girl, just six years old.

The gypsies came into the village to sell their wares, rugs piled high on their van. Piled so high you thought the little van might topple. They pulled up, and the man got out. The door in the side of the van slid open and a dozen children gurgled out, leaving a mattress and bedding clearly visible behind them. The gypsy's wife climbed down from the passenger seat, ignoring the children – headscarfed, a big woman, wearing long skirts, stretching and yawning. When they arrived in the village, Manolis saw them passing the window and expelled a loud 'Ha!', and little Eleni ran to the casement to look out. He had wanted a rug for the sitting room, where the stone floor was cold during the winter. When he announced that he was going to get a rug from the gypsy, Marina was a little surprised. They didn't have money for such things. Eleni was growing fast and needed a winter coat. She was still running around barefoot, and it was getting cooler. Marina mentioned this, quietly, but Manolis just scowled at them, and Eleni hid behind Marina's skirts.

Manolis approached the gypsy, showing all the signs that he intended to buy. Rug after rug was rolled out, and he exclaimed over the quality and the beauty of the patterns. The gypsy's wife hitched up her skirts to step barefoot on the carpets, to point out interesting parts of the design with words that held no sincerity. Her children ran in circles around the square. Vasso, whose kiosk was tiny back then, a wooden pillbox selling cigarettes and matches and not much else, put up the shutters to save her windows from any potential damage, and to stop stealthy hands from making quick grabs.

After half the rugs were spread out on the square, the gypsy man assured Manolis that the rest, still piled on his van, were duplicates, and that he had seen the full selection. Manolis held up a hand for the man to wait and popped back inside to take a bottle of ouzo and a couple of glasses from the shelf above the fireplace. Eleni dropped back from the window and Marina immediately knew he was up to no good.

Back in the square, Manolis sat down in the middle of a large rug, glasses and ouzo in hand, whilst the gypsy looked on in astonishment. Manolis declared the choice was so rich that he needed a drink to relax him so he could make his decision, and would he, the gypsy, care to join him in a glass? The gypsy, not wanting to offend and lose the sale – nor, indeed, ever having said no to a free drink in his life – obliged, and a conversation was struck up about this and that. Before long, Manolis, as smooth as you like, took out his cards and began shuffling them absentmindedly. He found a topic of conversation that the gypsy was passionate about.

Marina, who watched from the corner of the house with Eleni peeping from behind her skirts, seemed to recall it was football.

Whilst the gypsy was ranting, Manolis dealt him a hand, and whilst he was enthusing on some point of a recent match, Manolis, with his cards in his hand and a nod of his head, indicated to the gypsy to pick up the cards dealt him, which, with the ouzo doing its job, he did with no conscious thought, on automatic pilot, still talking. That was how the game started. Before the gypsy knew where he was, wagers of cigarettes were made, then the odd coin, until finally the gypsy had half his rugs staked against Manolis's 'grandfather's solid-gold watch', which

Marina knew was only gold plated, and which Manolis had been given for his eighteenth birthday. He said he had never liked it, fob watches being for old people.

But what the gypsy had not reckoned on was Manolis's cunning and, Marina suspected, his sleight of hand. Manolis lost persistently when the stakes were low, and just enough to keep the gypsy interested as they grew. But as the final hand was played, Marina knew the outcome before the gypsy suspected a thing.

The children were shouted back into the van, receiving cuffs for no reason. The gypsy's wife huffed and mumbled and pointed a wagging finger at her man, who responded by threatening her with the back of his hand. In less than a minute they were gone, leaving the square carpeted like a mosque.

Manolis slapped his hands together then, and rubbed them, grinning. Vasso took down her shutters and opened the kiosk again, and Manolis put his hands on his hips, leaned his head back, filled his lungs, and at the top of his voice shouted that he had very cheap rugs for sale.

Eleni looked up at Marina, puzzled, but Marina could not explain it to her in a way that would not show Manolis in a bad light, and so she said nothing.

Whilst the villagers disapproved of Manolis's carryings-on as a rule, they were not wealthy and were always keen to pick up a bargain. Manolis sold all but one of his entire stock of rugs within a couple of hours, at ridiculously cheap prices, and everyone, except the poor gypsies, was very happy.

After straightening the kicked rug, Marina suddenly took action and pushed and shoved the furniture aside, and rolled up the rug. She pulled it by one end through the kitchen, out into the courtyard and through the gate. She left it on the edge of the square where a gypsy could pick it up and sell it on to some unsuspecting villager. A full circle.

It was after she dumped the rug, on returning to the courtyard, that she noticed the door to the outhouse was open a crack. This was Manolis's domain, and no women or children were allowed. She tentatively pushed the door ajar, feeling fear, as Manolis's being dead didn't quite feel real yet. Maybe he was still in there? There was a smell of must and mothballs, oil and stale smoke. She felt for the light switch, to find it encrusted with dirt. She clicked it on and wiped her fingers on her apron.

Her eyes adjusted and her jaw dropped open. The room was full of farming tools and fishing nets, magazines, and coffee cups with mouldy fur lids covering their half-drunk contents. There were leather jackets on hangers over hooked nails in the ceiling beams, and one corner was full of crates of wine. There was a stack of new shoes in boxes, and bundles of shepherd's crooks, a row of paint tins, a tower of hats, six or seven foot pumps, a flock of lamps on top of a cupboard, a team of skittles…

Every surface was stacked to the ceiling, and there was barely room to get in.

Marina took a second to contemplate it all and then fought her way to the door on the other side of the room that faced the square. She drew the bolts and shoved it open. She called to a neighbour to spread the word through the village that Manolis's things were going the same way they came in – on the cheap. The villagers first turned up out of curiosity but soon came to buy. A scrum ensued and Marina provided coffee and biscuits. After a few days the piles dwindled, but still the villagers came. Rather than disappoint them, Marina began to buy replacements for popular items and so her shop was born.

It wasn't planned, but from then on the girls always had winter coats and summer and winter shoes, even if they chose not to wear them. Life proved easier without Manolis and they grew to be relatively comfortable. When Marina added food to her shop's offerings she also grew fat. Twenty years on her feet behind a counter full of sweets would account for the swollen ankles.

Years later, long after Manolis died, Eleni, now attending secondary school in Saros, brought up the subject of the gypsies and the rugs, and this time Marina gave a full account. Eleni, ever sensitive, was left without words and she retreated to her room, only to be enticed out hours later with a tray of freshly baked biscuits. When she emerged, she announced she was going to be a policewoman when she grew up, and Marina's heart sank at the thought of her eldest leaving home, perhaps posted to some distant province…

Marina wiggles her toes. Her shoes do look a bit worn. Although comfortable now, financially, she has not lost the inclination to be frugal, but perhaps it's time to break in her new ones. She should have brought them. The cat continues by her side right up to the first step. The steps! There are at least as many as she recalls, and they are just as steep as she remembers! The cat runs up the first flight, where it meets with other cats halfway, sprawled under the shade of a eucalyptus tree on the cool of the smooth, worn marble. They bump heads in greeting and the newcomer offers a lick here and there.

Marina looks up past the cats until, there at the top, with windows on three sides, she sees the apartment Aunt Efi rented. Marina's mouth twists. It could have been yesterday, so little has changed – this side of the house rising so tall from the old riverbed, the rear of the house settled into the side of the hill at the top of the steps. Like the prow of a boat, it juts over the ravine. She remembers the hours she spent looking out of the window, wishing her days away.

At the top of the steps, Marina recalls, a little way past the house, is a shop in someone's front room. If it is still there they will have cool water.

Marina changes hands with her bag and hitches her black skirt above her knees to begin the slow ascent. Her knees are fleshy and white, and she lowers her skirt just enough so she cannot see them, and begins.

'Just take it steady, Marina. There is no hurry. One step at a time. Next time better bring some drinking water. You have walked a long way already. Just take it steady, old girl.' Marina chuckles to herself. 'Not so much of the old. Forty-nine is no longer considered old, just a little worn, perhaps! Three, four, five, rest. Take a breath. A little rest. OK, ready? One, two, three, rest again. No need to race. Oh my…' She turns to see her progress and finds she has not come very far.

'OK, here we go again – one, breathe, two, breathe, three, four, five, rest.' Marina sets a rhythm and makes some steady progress.

She continues until she catches up with the cats. She bends to stroke them and considers how wise they are to rest halfway up the climb. Marina turns to sit on a step for a moment or two. She puts her hand out behind her and lowers herself steadily down. But the step is further than she thinks. Her hand reaches, but meets only air. She topples backward. Her head hits the rounded edge of the step and she sinks.

'Hello? Are you OK?'

Who is speaking? The voice sounds kind.

'No, don't try to move, just stay still a while. Are you OK? I think you must have fallen.'

Surely that is Eleni's voice? Could she be here? Marina feels a hand on her arm, soft, gentle. She strokes it. Little Eleni, such tiny fingers. No, that was then, when she was small. But her hands are still delicate. Eleni – she longs to be close to her again, like they were when Eleni was just a girl.

'Stay still a minute. No hurry. Slowly.'

It sounds like Eleni. How did she know she was here? She hopes she is not cross with her for being here. Hopes she will not shout and stomp around and call her interfering. Precious Eleni.

'I think you have banged your head. Steady! OK? Lean against me.' Marina feels a body sit next to her and move close to give support, an arm across her shoulders.

She slowly opens her eyes and blinks to focus. A small face looks back. She starts. 'Oh! Who are you?'

'It's OK, you've had a fall. How do you feel?'

Marina looks around for Eleni. 'Are you alone? Where's El–'

'Yes, just me. Do you want me to get someone, a doctor?'

'No! No doctor. There was no one else here?'

'Were you with someone?'

Marina puts her hand up to stroke the back of her head, which is throbbing, and it comes away streaked with blood.

'Oh, you are bleeding! I will get a doctor.' The girl makes a move to jump up, but Marina puts the bloodied hand on her arm.

'I don't need a doctor, but thank you.' Marina focuses her eyes and looks around her. The cats are still sprawled in the shade. The sun feels hot. She needs a drink and she needs to lie down. She wonders where she will stay.

'Look, I live just there.' The girl points to a whitewashed wall with a blue door at the bottom of the steps. A tiled roof can just be seen over the top of the wall. 'If you think you can make it, you can sit a while and I'll get you some water.'

Marina looks about her, judging how best to stand. The girl takes her by the arm but then changes her mind and lets go. She stands in front of Marina, puts her toes on Marina's toes and offers both her hands.

'One, two, three.' The girl leans back and Marina leans forward, and she rises gracefully.

'Well, that was easy.' Marina finds a smile.

'Practised on my gran.' The girl crosses herself and picks up Marina's bag.

With support, Marina makes it to the house. Through the blue door there is a shady garden full of orange and lemon trees, and a flower border against the walls on all sides. The girl guides Marina to a table and chairs under a pomegranate tree which is growing from the centre of a little paved courtyard.

'Sit here and I'll get some water.' She bounces up a couple of steps and into the house. Marina can see her head moving past the windows in succession, each room leading off the next. She stops by the last window and Marina hears glasses clinking.

'Do you live here with your mother?' Marina calls through the open window.

'No.' The girl crosses herself three times. 'Mum and Dad are dead.' Marina can hear in her accent that she is from the north – Thessaloniki, perhaps. 'We've got the house and the boat to ourselves for a year, my fiancé and me. His friend has gone to America, and then – well, it depends if there's work. If there's not, then God only knows where we will go.'

'Is he from the island, your fiancé?'

'Yup, born and bred.'

The girl returns with a tray. Iced water, cake and a damp cloth.

'Oh, thank you.' Marina feels quite overcome by the girl's kindness, and the thought of food and water brings clarity.

'My name's Irini.' She hands Marina the wet cloth for her head.

'Marina. Pleased to meet you.' Marina is reviving with the water and the cool, damp cloth.

Irini is small – a little waif, Marina decides, like her Eleni in many ways, except Eleni's hair is long. Both slim, long-limbed and agile, impish, but now Eleni's impishness has turned into anger. Marina wishes she knew why. So closed and secretive that it was almost a relief when she took herself, so young, off to Piraeus to join the port police.

With a drink of water and a piece of cake inside her, Marina begins to gather her thoughts and reminds herself why she is on the island. Irini's boyfriend is from the island. She can rule him out as he is engaged, but maybe he's the right age? She

33

decides to be more subtle than she was at the port with the donkey man. Irini is clearly a modern girl, and her fiancé will be the same age as her, or thereabouts. Hers is obviously not an arranged marriage to an older man – thank goodness those days are over. Marina sighs.

'How old are you, Irini?' she asks.

'Twenty-five.' Marina rules him out. She is only interested in men aged thirty-five.

Her own girls are twenty-three and twenty-eight. To Marina it makes no sense that the younger one has been married twice and Eleni not yet once. But, she reflects, there is hope now, God willing. It was such a happy moment when Eleni told her that she had asked to be stationed on the island because she had met someone who was important to her. Marina's relief at this news eclipsed any other thoughts.

Irini smiles at her. She is feeding pieces of cake to a stray cat that has followed them into the garden. She has a smile like Eleni's.

For Eleni, this was a rare opening up, and Marina responded carefully. All she said to Eleni was, 'How wonderful, darling, I am so happy for you. I hope you will be very happy. How old is he?' And she stepped towards Eleni and dared to stroke her hair. 'Thirty-five,' Eleni snapped, and batted her hand away. Marina swallowed hard at this reply, but she tried even harder with Eleni, saying, 'Oh darling, I am so pleased for you, especially as you are still not too old to have children.' She brought out the ouzo to toast Eleni and her young man. But Eleni stood up abruptly, sending the chair crashing, and stormed from the room. She went back to Piraeus the same day.

Marina sighs. She didn't understand Eleni's actions then and she doesn't understand them now. Eleni saddens her. So sweet when she was little. Eight was a difficult time – any time, a difficult time – to lose your dad. Stupid man. What a ridiculous way to die.

Irini takes the cloth that Marina is holding against her head. Irini bends to inspect the wound and pats and dabs gently until the sticky blood is out of Marina's short hair.

'It looks OK to me. It has stopped bleeding, but I guess you should rest or something. Where are you staying?' She is up and moving again, not one to keep still.

Marina wishes she had Irini's energy to run the shop. The hours are long and she is grateful that Costas from across the road works for her in the afternoons so she can catch up on her sleep. The evenings feel the longest, from six until about eleven thirty. Then the shop becomes her sitting room, with visitors, a television on the wall and a spare chair for friends. But often she is alone for long periods. It's all very tiring. Yes, Irini's energy would help.

Marina yawns. 'Nowhere yet. Anywhere. Somewhere without tourist prices.' She giggles.

'What about Zoe's?' Irini points towards the wall at the far end of the garden and Marina sees a lichen-covered red-tiled roof peeking over the top a short distance away. 'She's as cheap as it gets here. She's bound to have room as she never advertises. Illegal, I guess.'

Marina stands and wobbles a little. Irini skips to her side.

'No, I am fine. Just tired,' Marina says.

'I'll come and introduce you. Let me take your bag.'

Irini gambols out of the garden door. Marina follows her to the house next door, which is built side-on to the path. The lower level looks shut up, as if used for storage. The first floor, at right angles to the path, has a balcony with a wrought-iron railing running along its length and several doors leading into the house. The gate, off the path they are on, hangs open, offering access to a gaily tiled courtyard liberally furnished with flowers in terracotta pots. A rickety iron staircase leads up to the first floor. The central door at the top is tall and ornately panelled. It was a grand house at one time. Over the decades layers of paint have rounded the panelled edges, and to Marina it looks organic. She runs her hand across it, thinking of the generations of people who have come and gone.

Irini pulls some weeds from a pot of flowers further along the balcony, and comes back to throw them out onto the path in the direction of her house just as Marina reaches the top step.

'Zoe hasn't the time to do everything.' Irini smiles, and knocks on the door.

Chapter 3

Muted, insincere voices doling out clichéd lines dominate the sounds coming from inside. The door is opened, a fist's width, by a middle-aged woman, grey around her temples, with a flat face, almond-shaped eyes and a wide mouth. Someone else turns down the television's drone.

'Yes?' She has a slight lisp but her voice is firm.

'Roula, let whoever it is in.' Roula turns to the person inside and Marina sees she has different-coloured bows in her hair at the back, at odd angles.

'But we don't know them.' Roula keeps hold of the door edge to stop it opening any further.

'Roula, just open the door, please.'

'It's me, Mrs Zoe. Irini.'

'There, you know Irini, open the door.'

'There's someone with her.' Roula opens the door wide and walks back inside, no longer concerned.

Inside is cool and dark. Dust hovers and swirls in the strips of sunlight streaming through the slats of half-closed shutters. At first glance everything seems white. The tall windows extend all along one wall and halfway along the adjacent wall, giving the impression of a conservatory. The room is divided by a beam running across the ceiling where a wall has presumably been removed. Beyond the visual divide, two stiff-backed sofas without arms and two matching chairs are arranged around a low table. Judging by the tidiness and the pristine condition of the furniture, which is clearly decades old, Marina presumes this part of the room is left 'for guests and best'.

'Come in, Irini, come in. I am just feeding Gran.' This must be Zoe.

Marina's eyes adjust and she takes in more detail. She can see that, next to a table in the middle of the room, a bony old woman is seated, her hands curled inward across her chest, one side of her face drooping. She is groaning quietly. Roula has taken a hard-backed chair by the wall and watches a television that is mounted on a bracket attached to the dividing beam. She has turned the sound up again and is immersed in the soap opera. There are several wooden chairs lined against the walls under the shuttered windows. On one of these is a large old lady leaning over to one side, her weight melting her into the seat, fast asleep. Near to her, on another chair in the corner, is a pile of clothes heaped haphazardly.

'Hi, Zoe. I have brought you a customer!' Zoe is standing in front of the woman by the table, a spoon in one hand, a bowl in the other.

'Ha, don't let the taxman hear you say that.' Zoe has a halo of white hair loosely knotted on top of her head. Her wrinkled eyes are moist and her creased mouth is soft. She catches a drip on the thin woman's chin with the spoon. She pauses and turns to Marina. 'You know how it is, can't afford to be legal, can't afford not to take people in. Pay for this certificate, pay for that legality, all before you've earned a drachma.'

'It's the euro now, Mum.' Roula corrects her without taking her eyes from the television. Zoe wipes one hand on the thin material of her clean white bib apron, through which the bold floral pattern of her shapeless dress can be seen.

'Can you turn that down a bit, please, Roula?'

'I love this programme, Mum.'

'Just a bit.' Zoe puts down her spoon and picks up the remote control, and turns it down.

'Aw, Mum!'

'Anyway, come in, come in, come in.'

'Mrs Zoe, this is Mrs Marina.' Irini uses the formal address of her mother tongue.

'Very pleased to meet you, Mrs Marina.' She wipes the thin lady's chin with the edge of her apron. 'This is my mum – we call her Gran for Roula. She had a stroke years ago. Recovered quite well, but another one five years back and, well… Before that I looked after houses for foreigners.' She sighs and puts a spoonful of food to her mother's open mouth.

Marina's memory returns to the documentary. Caretaking for the foreigners, the man said, was golden work. The camera zoomed in from a distant shot to a close-up of a very grand house. Americans, usually, he continued. Charmed by the island, they

39

bought holiday homes but then found the distance restricted their visits more than they had imagined. One or two just needed a housekeeper to hold the key in case of an emergency, plumbing, drains, and to get the house aired before they came. Even though the work was negligible they paid well.

'A nice job, I imagine?' Irini asks. Zoe smiles and nods.

Was it a nice job? Marina wonders. The documentary included an interview with a property manager. Many of the foreign owners rent their houses to other tourists when they are away, he said. So the keyholders get paid well for looking after them. They become responsible for the changeovers and the comfort of the paying guests.

Marina imagines the stresses of dealing with demanding guests, worried owners, lazy cleaners, and rejects it as a potential career choice...

'Yes, I would meet and greet the holidaymakers from the hydrofoil, and have a donkey man arranged to load their heavy bags, and charge a little extra on top of his pay, too.' Zoe lays the spoon across the bowl and puts some imaginary money in her back pocket, and chuckles at her own naughtiness, and shrugs as if to say 'needs must'.

'I would arrange the cleaners, and charge a little extra,' she continues with a twinkle in her eye. 'A little here, a little there...'

The documentary followed some new arrivals on their way to a villa, winding through a maze of narrow lanes. This reinforced their dependence on the keyholder, Marina thought, before they even set foot inside the property. The tourists would never be able to find the house on their own.

'But sometimes it was very stressful. If there were building works nearby it was a problem. If a donkey was too loud, a problem. If the air conditioning failed, a big problem. With some people, everything was wrong. Then it was hell.' But Zoe smiles at the memory.

'Mostly it was a wonderful, well-paid game,' Zoe concludes. 'I had a huge bunch of keys at my belt and all the neighbours wanted to know what they were for. They saw my work as a mystery. Back then there was only me doing it. Now there are more foreign owners and more keyholders. But when it was just me I was the only person on the island who knew who lived where, right across the island, both Greek and foreign. Still do, mostly.' Zoe takes a breath and finishes feeding her mother, putting down the bowl and spoon.

'I must be off. Come and see me when you're settled, Marina, and I'll show you round the island.' Irini puts Marina's bag on the floor as she leaves.

'So, what can I do for you, Mrs Marina?' Zoe asks.

'I need a room for a few days, nothing fancy, just somewhere to lay my head.'

Zoe gives the dish with the spoon to Roula, who passes them through a hatch without taking her eyes from the television. Zoe wipes her mother's mouth on her apron again and then wipes her own hands.

'Well, you won't find anything fancy here,' Zoe says.

There is a guttural chortle from the corner. Marina focuses on what she took to be a pile of clothes and which now reveals itself to be a diminutive man creased like an old newspaper. His jacket, too big for his scrawny frame, has slid off his shoulder down to his elbow.

'And your fancy days are over!' Zoe leans over to him and pulls his jacket back onto his shoulder and pats him on the back, smiling kindly, before turning to Marina again.

'My brother-in-law, Bobby,' she states, and continues without giving Marina time to acknowledge the introduction. 'There's a room two doors along.' She points towards the tall front door and indicates the way to turn. 'Shower, fridge, bed, balcony, sea view. No air conditioning, but there's a ceiling fan.' She opens a drawer under the table and rummages around until she finds the key. 'There you go.'

'Thank you, I need a little lie-down.'

'Yes, is time for Gran to lie down too.' Zoe walks behind her mother's chair.

'Right, well, I will go and get settled then. Nice to meet you all.'

But Zoe is already concentrating on manoeuvring the wheelchair. The large woman is still asleep in her chair, as is Bobby now in his, and Roula is talking to the man on the television. Zoe's mother grunts at her.

Roula replies, 'Yes, I know, Gran – have a good sleep.' To Marina, the grunts are indecipherable.

The balcony belonging to Marina's room overlooks the courtyard. Marina can see the sparkling deep blue of the sea and the purple hills of the mainland beyond. That amazing view across the water, dotted with islands, takes her breath away all over again, and she wonders why she doesn't take little breaks from the shop more often.

The heavy iron key fits snugly in the old lock and speaks of age and faded glory. The door is tall, but not quite as grand as the one into Zoe's rooms. This room, with its high ceiling, is charming and clean, scrubbed white. A corner is sectioned off for a shower and toilet. The shower tray is cracked but both the shower and the toilet are clean. Marina doesn't bother to look in the fridge. She wearily slides her feet across to open the window onto a balcony at the back, which is big enough for one chair. It overlooks the top of the town and offers a view of the island's interior, right up to the top where pine trees crown the ridge. She is much wearier than she realised.

She shuffles back to sit on the bed to test its softness, and to her relief it is firm. Her back feels fine at the moment, but a soft bed might set it off. She pushes the heel of one shoe down with the toe of the other and kicks it off. The second shoe follows. Her feet feel slightly swollen. She bends her knee to bring her foot up to reach her hand and rolls off a black sock. Her feet feel much better for the air. She unties

43

the satin bow at the neck of her blouse and unbuttons the front. It has done well for its years. She unbuttons the cuffs and hangs the blouse on the back of the door. It looks a little more grey than black now, but, after twenty years of washing it, Marina is not surprised.

She switches on the ceiling fan, rummages in her bag for paper and a pen and flops onto the bed in her support bra and skirt. She lies for a while and wonders how many men aged thirty-five, born on the island, will still be living here.

'There could be hundreds, and there's only three months before Eleni is here.' She shifts and manoeuvres herself onto her stomach. She hopes Costas is managing the shop on his own.

'Now, girl, let's concentrate, don't be panicking. How many men aged thirty-five will there be on the island? The documentary said that the island's population, without tourism, was about three thousand.' Marina writes it down.

'So a third of them will be old, say over seventy. And a third will be young, say under twenty, so that leaves one thousand.' She writes this down and puts too many zeros, and scribbles it out and then writes it correctly.

'Half of them will be women so...' She carefully divides by two. 'Five hundred men between twenty and seventy.' She writes this down.

'Now, let's think, there are' – she uses her fingers to help – 'five decades from twenty to seventy.' She writes this down and giggles at her progress. 'Fives into one thousand. So there are twenty, no, two hundred men between the age of thirty and forty. Oh my goodness, so many. But there are ten years in a decade, divided by the ten, twenty men that will be thirty-five. Still, that's a lot!'

She turns over the paper and writes the numbers one to twenty down the edge. Next to one she adds *Yanni – donkey man*.

The pen and paper are abandoned on the bedside table and Marina manages a low, ungainly roll and twist and flops onto her back. She pretends the slow waft of the fan on the ceiling is cooling. She watches its rotations. A fly comes in through the window and buzzes around the room before heading towards the fan. Marina waits for it to be buffeted by the air current but instead it flies under the fan and lands gently on one of the blades.

'A fat lot of good that is!'

The fly sits for a moment before buzzing off to explore Marina's blouse, and then, just as suddenly, it is out of the window. Marina can feel her eyes closing. The fan motor whirs and she is lulled to sleep.

Chapter 4

It is not much cooler when she awakes. She can tell she hasn't slept as long as she normally does. The fan still turns slowly and there is a gentle breeze coming through the window.

Marina sits up and sees the paper she has written on by her bed, with *Yanni – donkey man* at the top. She decides there is no time like the present, and rolls on her socks and eases her feet, now somewhat less swollen, into her shoes. They are comfortable once they are on. She rubs the front of the shoes with her fingers to take off some of the dust. The heat dries everything, dust everywhere. It is the same at the shop.

She positions her feet on the floor and, with her hands on her knees, rolls her weight forward to stand. Her back feels fine. She stretches, adjusts her bra straps, which cut a little on the shoulders, and picks her blouse off the hook on the door. It feels cool to the touch. It slips on like silk and she buttons it up and tucks it in her nondescript black skirt and adjusts it until she feels respectable.

The view out of the window up to the ridge catches her attention, and she wonders how long it will take her and if she is fit enough.

She looks in her big bag, puts her hand in and touches the contents tenderly before she pushes it under the bed and leaves with just her small bag, in which she has her purse, her list of one name, her pencil and the key to her room.

The balcony view takes her breath away again. Marina stands for a moment, taking in the sea and the whitewashed houses. She feels proud to be Greek.

As she walks along the balcony she can hear voices.

'I know, Roula.' It is Zoe's voice.

'But Mum, you can't leave her like that. It's not right!' Roula's voice is loaded with emotion.

'Why didn't you tell me we had run out?' Zoe sounds tired.

'I didn't know. How was I meant to know?' Roula sounds angry this time.

'Well, you were the last person to get one from the cupboard. Didn't you notice?' Zoe's pitch is rising, the words coming out faster.

Marina begins to tiptoe past the door, which has been left ajar.

'No, I just put my hand in and grabbed one. It's my fault, isn't it? Sorry, Mum, sorry, sorry, Roula's sorry.' Roula starts to cry, big heaving sobs. Marina pauses.

'No, my love, it is not your fault. Look, the order came today and Yanni will bring them over tonight. What else can I do? I can't leave you on your own for that long to go and get them myself. It's too much for even you, my love.' Zoe finds her patience, and her words come out soothing and calm.

'I'll be fine, Mum. You treat me like a baby sometimes – I am forty-two, you know.' Roula sniffs but doesn't seem to be able to stop crying.

'You are forty-one, not forty-two until next month, and I do not treat you like a baby. I just don't want to ask too much of you. God knows I couldn't manage without you.' Zoe exhales loudly.

Marina knocks very quietly.

'Mum, there's someone at the door.' Roula is still crying and continues muttering, 'It's my fault, it's my fault.'

'I didn't hear anyone. Hello?' Zoe's voice approaches the door.

Marina pushes the door open. The dust swirls in the shaft of sunshine that enters.

'Hello. I hope I'm not interrupting?' There is a curious smell in the room as the door opens. Roula is wiping her eyes and, with one foot in front of the other, is rocking back and forth and watching the television with the sound off. The large lady is asleep. Her dribbling glistens in the sun the open door has let in, and someone has put a handkerchief under her chin to protect her clothes. Marina can hear the old thin lady groaning from the next room.

'No, she won't be all right on her own, Gran,' Zoe calls to her. 'Hello, Mrs Marina. Is everything OK?' Her eyes widen at the thought that the room may not be acceptable to Marina, as she has already allocated the money Marina will pay. 'Is anything wrong? Do you need anything extra?' Tears well in her eyes.

'No, no, everything is fine, the room is lovely. I just wondered if I could be of any help.'

Zoe lets out a little laugh of relief.

'I just need to be three people at once! No, we are fine. Thank you.' The smell is getting stronger, and Marina wonders if there is something wrong with the drains, but the smell is fresher than that, if fresh is the right word.

'Look, if you need to go somewhere I can stay here for you, no problem.' Marina takes a step into the room.

'Oh my goodness, no, I would not dream of it! No, Gran will be fine, we just have to wait a while until Yanni gets here. Our order came today.' Zoe takes a step back and puts an arm around Roula, whose sobbing is quietening. 'Yanni picks things up from the port and drops them off at his store on his way home in the afternoon, and then when he starts work again in the evening he will pick them up and bring them over here. We'll be fine.'

Her mother groans quite loudly from next door, and the sound echoes slightly, indicating that the room is largely empty. Zoe turns her head to the open door, the shadows beyond showing nothing, then turns to Roula.

'She says she is sorry.' Roula seems to be the interpreter.

'Gran, you have no reason to be sorry. It is not your fault. That's just the way life is. Besides, we are just swapping. You changed me when I was a baby and now it's my turn.' Zoe smiles and listens, and her mother laughs, little staccato wisps of air escaping the back of her throat. Zoe's shoulders relax.

'Can I go for you?' Marina asks.

'Do you know the island? His store is right across the other side of town.'

'No, not really.'

'Then you would never find it.' Zoe looks out of the door across the maze of white-walled houses and the alleys running between them.

'Then let me stay. You go, I'll be fine.' Marina takes another step inside.

'Yes, let her stay.'

Marina jumps at the voice behind her. It is Bobby. She hasn't noticed him there, he is sunk so low in his chair. He winks at Marina, a sly grin which lights his eyes.

'It's not right, I wouldn't dream of it. You are a guest,' Zoe says.

'Don't be silly. How long will it take you?' Marina steps across and stands beside Bobby's chair.

'Well, it will take up to forty minutes, if I don't meet anyone on the way…' Marina can see that Zoe is tempted.

'That's nothing. Go. We'll be here when you get back,' Marina says.

'On your way, Zoe.' Bobby is chuckling.

'We'll be fine,' Marina says, and to demonstrate she pulls Bobby's jacket back onto his shoulder and sits down next to him.

'OK, then, if you are sure.' Zoe disappears into the back room. She can be heard talking to her mother. 'I will just leave this sheet over you. Yes, I know it is hot in here. Do you want the shutters open? No. OK. I'll be as quick as I can.'

'Not often I get a pretty lady sitting next to me these days,' Bobby says as Zoe comes back into the room.

'Uncle Bobby, you behave yourself. Marina, I will be as fast as I can.'

'Oh, it's *Three, Two, One, Three, Two, One*.' Roula holds up her hand showing three fingers, then two and then one. 'I love this programme. *Three, Two, One*.'

'Roula! I won't be long, OK?'

'*Three, Two, One*. Yes, fine, bye. *Three, Two, One*.' Roula turns the sound on and sings along to the theme tune.

'Right then.' Zoe hesitates, then turns and marches down the stairs. She leaves the door open and the sun streams in.

Chapter 5

'So what's the story?' Uncle Bobby asks. Marina feels he would be shuffling up closer if only his body would respond. She feels a little ashamed that she is glad he cannot move much. He feels dangerous enough with his tone of voice, his manner of speaking and that glint in his eye.

'What? Sorry, what story?' Marina wishes she had chosen a chair a little further away, but continues to sit beside him, staring blankly at the television.

'You. Why are you here?' Bobby is chuckling as he speaks.

'I needed a room and Zoe needed someone to stay whilst–'

'My body may be knackered but I am not crackers!' He laughs out loud at his joke. The laughter comes tensely, in a series of croaks. It sounds rather as if he is clearing his throat. He sucks in some air, wheezing. Now he coughs and asks, 'Not here in this room, I mean here on the island?' He tuts at her as if she is a naughty child being purposefully awkward. 'I have never seen anyone look less like a tourist, and you are not here visiting family or you would be staying with them, so, come on my girl, what's the story?' Marina casts a sideways glance at him, long enough to see his eyes are shining, that all the life he has left is eager to play.

'Oh, I see,' Marina says, surprised at how coy her voice sounds, and fiddles with the bow on her blouse. She wishes she had the shop counter in front of her. She feels strangely vulnerable next to Bobby.

'Come on, spill the beans, pretty lady. Are you on a mission or do you have a private liaison?' He shuts his mouth abruptly.

Marina turns to face him to see if he is serious. He has shuffled over slightly and she is startled to see his face so close. The shadowed room is kind to his features, stripping back the years with shadows of obscurity. He has long eyelashes, and his eyes are kind and full of fun. His gaze bores into her and she feels he can see her soul. His nose is so straight, chiselled – she thinks how clichéd this description is – but it is his mouth that is dangerous. Promises, suggestions, lingering in the way the muscles move around his mouth, the tone of voice, as if he knows every trick and he has caught you already. For an old man his hair is still dark and lustrous.

He moves a little and the sun catches him through the lattice shutters, dashing a streak of light across his face, illuminating all the crevices and wrinkles. His age returns in the sunlight. Her fear of him is dispelled along with the passing illusion of youth. She exhales and answers him.

'A private liaison – I would say not!' She is glad to hear her voice back to normal, and she laughs at the idea that anyone could think she might be engaged in a liaison. She relaxes a little on her chair, her back no longer so upright.

'Ah, so you are on a mission!' Bobby chuckles. He is thoroughly enjoying himself, like a lion prowling through the undergrowth of words.

'A mission of mercy!' Marina joins him in adopting a bantering tone.

'So, a mission of mercy, is it? You are here to save someone?' He slowly raises his hand, shaking and unsure, and scratches his nose. 'From someone else or from themselves?'

Marina considers this.

'I am here to save someone, or two people, actually, from an unsuitable match.' She ends the sentence with a nod of conclusion. But her mind wanders off. Eleni stormed out after Marina asked about his age. She went to pack a suitcase. But before she left she called her lover. The tones were hushed and whispered, a cupped hand to her mouth. There was something in the tone that Marina had not heard for a long time. She heard a peace, a contentment that made her feel such joy for her offspring. She lingered behind the door, not to eavesdrop on what was being said – indeed, she couldn't hear anything much – but to capture more of Eleni's tone. Whoever it was gave Marina hope that Eleni was going to be fine. Unless…

'And you would know the pain of an unsuitable match because you have been there yourself, perhaps, and know the pain it causes, the years of emptiness, the wasted youth?' Bobby puts an overdramatic tone into his voice, inviting a dramatic reply or, perhaps, a complete dismissal. He gets neither.

'Now, how would you figure that?' Her shoulders droop at his observation, despite the light-hearted way in which it was delivered.

Bobby drops his tone and, instead, compassion enters his voice. 'Well, you have been in mourning for a good long time – that is not the latest fashion.' He juts his chin at her blouse. Mania flushes and makes a mental note to buy another one when the man with his van next comes to her village. 'And the only person worth mourning for that length of time would be your husband, and for him to be dead you must have married an older man when you were very young. Or else I am wrong and he was just plain unlucky. But my guess is he was not unlucky, as he had you as a wife!' He laughs gently and his eyes are kind. He winks at her again.

'You cheeky thing! Actually he was both older and unlucky.' Marina cannot decide if she likes Bobby or not.

'So, one thing at a time. How much older?' he asks. Marina realises he probably sits in that chair all day, every day, with the same company and only the television to distract him. She sits in her shop with different people coming and going all day long, but it doesn't stop her feeling bored sometimes. She cannot imagine what it must be like for him. She feels lucky. She is happy to give him a bit of her life story to entertain him, despite the fact that he is clearly a rogue at heart.

'Well, I was fourteen when I became engaged.' She pauses and looks up at the ceiling. It is painted white and is composed of an intricate cross-hatch of latticework as decoration. 'You know, I can still remember the engagement party. It was at his family house.' She glances at Bobby to see if she is holding his interest. He urges her on with a nod of his head. 'I knew the family, of course – everyone did. But there were three of them – three brothers, that is – and I could not tell them apart. You can't when you are that age, can you? At that age old people all look the same.' She looks back at her lap and fiddles with her wedding ring. 'He wasn't that old, really, he just seemed so to me at the time. He was thirty-six. A few months later, when we were married, I had just turned fifteen.' Marina sighs.

She remembers the dress her mother made for her to wear. It was too hot for the weather, the neckline too high. She brushed her hair smooth and her mother came in and sat on her bed, and brushed it some more as she stood looking out of the window, trying to see the house they were going to across the village in the dark night. Marina could see her mother's face reflected in the windowpane. It looked strange, almost as if she was scared, or very sad. Marina realised later, when she had her own children, that it was the thought of a child losing her innocence that was reflected in her mother's eyes that night.

Her mother stayed with her in her room until it was time to go to the engagement party. 'I can remember at the party I was so scared, so nervous, I couldn't look up. I just looked at the floor. People were coming up to me and congratulating me and patting me on the shoulders but I kept looking at the floor. When I got home I still had no idea which one it was that I was engaged to.'

'Land?' Bobby asks.

Marina nods. A picture of the village house where she grew up comes to mind, with its rough stone walls and packed-earth yard where chickens pecked at worms and beetles. Her parents toiled thankless hours in the hot sun, planting potatoes and picking grapes for a labourer's wage. They owned a little land but it wasn't big enough on its own to make a living – not big enough unless they could merge with the land belonging to the farmer next door, Manolis's father.

The family had moved to a nearby town briefly, just before the merger, and Marina's parents got jobs in offices. But then cuts came, and Marina's mother lost her job. Soon after that, they returned to the village.

'Ah, so not for love, then?'

'No, not for love. Just the same old tale of many women in Greece.'

'A fine woman like you needs love.' Bobby shuffles in his seat and his jacket falls off his bony shoulder again. Marina pulls it back on. His face is back in the shadows and she can picture him in his youth, and she smiles.

'We all need love,' she answers.

'So, did you find love?' Bobby gives her a lingering look.

'What, with Manolis? Ha! There were times when I was fond of him, but I think I was just used to him being around. He wasn't exactly what you might call a good provider! He was never home much.'

Marina's mind reels at the recall of all the mad schemes Manolis engaged himself in. He always had something on the go, some iron in the fire. Just putting his back into an honest day's labour in his olive groves was not his style. The olives suffered from the lack of attention and the crops dwindled, so his search for alternative sources of money became more and more frantic.

'Here's a story that will describe my "loving" husband to you.' Marina feels Bobby settle, ready to be transported.

She relates the story of one of his first enterprises, when he diddled his brothers out of the family fishing boat in a game of cards combined with a large amount of whisky. The brothers were invited to dinner with his new wife and they came to taste her cooking. Marina and her mother baked all day so as not to disappoint, and the brothers relished every mouthful.

After dinner, out came the whisky, and Marina took herself off to the kitchen to wash up and generally stay out of the way. Manolis played the generous host, inventing toast after toast, until out slipped his cards, and before the brothers knew where they were they were involved in a riotous game, first betting for this and that old bit of furniture, then on to betting olive trees one by one until whole orchards had passed hands. Finally, everything was put into a pot and the deal was the sole ownership of the family fishing boat which, as things stood, they took turns to use. If you have a fishing boat you always eat; it was a heavy bet.

This was the first time Marina saw Manolis pull this card-game trick and she thought it was just how the boys behaved. It was only later she found out that he had used sleight of hand, as well as a lot of whisky, against his own family. She lost all trust in him that day. She was his wife but he treated her as a maid, to cook and clean for him. And if he could treat his brothers in this way, how could she imagine he would be any more loyal to her? Before the marriage ink was dry, they had grown apart.

He swapped the traditional wooden fishing boat for a big covered hulk of a vessel with no seagoing capability, and the villagers laughed. His brothers ranted. It was his friend who put him up to it, Mitsos. Even his mother said that Manolis and Mitsos were trouble, from the moment they learnt to walk in the village square together.

Manolis and Mitsos spent weeks working on that old boat, gutting the insides and installing padded seats and a fancy music system, and divulging the details of their plan to no one. The villagers thought they had gone mad, and came to see the work in progress and to poke fun. Were they planning to woo the fish into the boat with music from the speakers, or did they expect them to die laughing?

Bobby is chuckling away by this point and encourages Marina to continue her narrative. She is a little sad that she has no need to embellish. The truth is ridiculous enough.

When he painted the whole thing pink, Marina thought she might never leave the house again, lest she die of shame. And when they manhandled the barge into the water, Manolis pulling at the front, and Mitsos pushing at the back, the whole village turned out to help, and to watch it sink. But it stayed afloat, and they slowly towed it through a calm sea to a nearby town behind a borrowed rowing boat. The village children ran along the shore shouting and jeering until they reached the town.

There, Manolis and Mitsos stocked the shelves inside with glasses and bottles and put up a sign outside which read *The Love Boat*. People stopped laughing then, as young tourists filled the boat night after night.

The villagers were kind to Marina, who was seven months pregnant with Eleni then, with Manolis out night after night running his floating bar. At least they had money for a while. But like everything else Manolis did it all turned sour, and he got crosser and crosser, and they were penniless again within months.

'But I got used to being on my own.' Marina closes her mouth and lets her hands, which have been assisting with the telling of the tale, rest in her lap.

'Well, if he left you alone I would be calling him foolish, not unlucky!'

'Well, we must call him unlucky because it does nobody any good to speak ill of the dead, and it really was a ridiculous way that he died.' Marina becomes grave and picks imaginary bits of fluff off her black skirt.

'We've all got to go sometime, and we all have to die of something. Not everything is curable. I keep my hopes up.' Bobby sounds cheerful.

'What, that they will find a cure for you?' Marina asks.

'No! That I'll die before they do find a cure! I don't want to become even more of a burden to Zoe! She has enough with *Yiayia* and Roula, never mind taking care of Aunt Eleftheria and me.' He nods towards the large sleeping woman.

They both look at Eleftheria, who remains motionless, snoring ever so quietly.

'Ah. They should make it longer! *Three, Two, One. Three, Two, One.* Does anyone want some water?' Roula is up and jigging to the closing music.

Marina has forgotten she is there.

'Yes, please, Roula.' Bobby shifts in his seat.

'Do you need a hand?' Marina asks.

'No, thanks. *Yiayia*?' Roula raises her voice. 'Do you want some water?' There is a low sound from the room beyond, and Roula takes some glasses from

61

a cupboard and fills them from a plastic bottle by the door.

'I can't understand a word Zoe senior says. Zoe can't understand a lot of what she says either, although she pretends she can. But Roula has whole conversations with her,' Bobby whispers to Marina.

Roula puts a glass of water on the table for each of them.

'Oh brilliant, I love this!' Marina follows Roula's gaze, which is again fixed on the screen, now showing a Turkish soap opera badly dubbed into Greek. The synchronisation is so bad that the man looks like he is speaking the woman's words, and vice versa. Marina laughs. Roula tells her to 'Shh', and sits enraptured.

Marina indicates the water and asks Bobby if he needs a hand, and he nods. She puts it to his lips and lets him drink before taking a drink of her own.

'So did he die by the might of God, or the might of man?' Bobby asks, licking water from his lips.

'Who?' Marina looks at Bobby and back to the television to see if she has missed something. She doesn't know the series and has no idea who he is talking about.

'No, your husband, you dizzy flower,' Bobby says.

'Oh, him. It was another daft idea he had with Mitsos. They were always scheming to make money. The last scam was fishing. Using dynamite. They thought they were so clever. Drop the dynamite in the water, boom…' Marina adds some hand gestures to bring to life the image of the explosion, spilling water on her skirt. It feels cool as it soaks through to her thigh. 'And the dead fish float to the surface, and you gather them in a net.' Marina sighs wearily. 'So they were at Mitsos's house getting ready for the first trial, and they bound this dynamite up in a package, and as a joke Manolis threw it to Mitsos and said – and these were his last words, mind you – "English rugby!" So Mitsos threw the dynamite back and Manolis missed the catch and that was that. Mitsos lost one arm and three fingers off his other hand, and an eye. I lost my husband, and Eleni and Artemis lost their father.' Marina's voice is very matter-of-fact.

'Oh, I am sorry. That must have been hard.' Bobby shifts uncomfortably and his jacket begins another descent from his shoulder.

'Harder for the girls than me. I had grown wise to him. They still thought he was wonderful, swinging them in the air, telling them his mad schemes with such excitement. Poor girls – it is amazing more harm wasn't done.'

Roula stands up suddenly. 'He did it – him. I never liked him. I don't know why she is crying, he wasn't nice.' Roula is pointing to the man on the television and shouting to no one in particular. 'Good, it's finished, stupid programme.' She picks up the remote and surfs channels. 'Yes, brilliant! I love this.' She sits down again.

It is a cartoon dubbed into Greek, the voice weirdly accentuated, adults pretending to be children, pretending to be monsters.

63

'So, your mission here…?' Bobby has the teasing tone in his voice again.

'Ah yes, my mission here.' Marina shifts in her seat.

'Will it be a straightforward mission, or will there be some jiggery-pokery?' He chuckles and begins to cough. Marina helps him drink some more water.

Whilst she is close to him she looks him in the eye and whispers, 'It is a mission of the utmost secrecy. My daughter will never forgive me if she finds out. I must move like a shadow and gather the facts before I know if I need to strike.' Marina puts the glass of water down and waves her fist as a dramatic end to her exaggerated speech, and rocks back, laughing.

'So, much jiggery-pokery, then! And how will you begin, or have you begun already?'

There is a moan from the back room.

'No, she's not back yet, *Yiayia*,' Roula calls.

'I have begun, but I am not sure how to continue. I need some help,' Marina says.

'Then I am your man!' Bobby's jacket slides even further off his shoulder and Marina hooks it back on. He twists his upper body a little to try to keep the jacket from sliding again.

'I think, Bobby, that perhaps you are not the man,' Marina says, patting him gently on the shoulder.

'How do you know? What help do you need?' Bobby looks offended.

Marina drops her voice to a whisper. 'What would be most helpful would be a list of all the men aged thirty-five on the island who have been here all their lives. But there will be no such list. I think I will need to gather from far and wide.'

'Like I said, I am your man!' Bobby says loudly.

'Bobby, I think that I need–' Marina is cut off.

'Hello, everyone, is everything all right?' Zoe clatters up the steps and comes through the door with a bundle of bags which she dumps on the table.

Roula drags her gaze from the television and hastens to the table, picking through the bags. Zoe puts the larger items away.

'Hi, *Yiayia*. I'll be in in a minute,' she calls to the back room. 'Everyone OK?' She puts a few items in the hatch through to the kitchen.

'Fine,' Marina answers.

'Have you been behaving yourself, you old rascal?' Zoe smiles at Bobby, who grins wickedly back but doesn't say a word. 'They had to lock their daughters up when he was a young man. A leopard never changes its spots, does it, Bobby?'

'*Tyropita* – cheese pies – yum! Is one for me? Can I have one, please – I am starving, please?' Roula is hopping from foot to foot.

'Quiet down – yes, of course there is one for you. I thought we could all have a little treat.' Zoe separates the cheese pies from the rest of her shopping.

'Right, well, I'll be off then. I had planned to go for a little walk and I don't want to leave it too late.' Marina looks through the door. It is late afternoon and the sun slants golden.

'Oh, I got you a pie too. Will you not stay and eat with us? Roula, wait until I have made some salad to

65

go with it, and we need to see to *Yiayia* first,' Zoe says.

'But I am hungry,' Roula replies.

'Thank you, Mrs Zoe, but I think I will take my walk. Bobby, it has been a pleasure. Roula, thank you for the water.' Marina turns to Aunt Eleftheria but she is still asleep.

'Well, take your pie with you. It is the least I can offer for your kindness,' Zoe says.

Marina's stomach responds appreciatively; she has only eaten a slice of Irini's cake since breakfast. 'Well, that's very kind of you. See you all later.'

No one replies. Roula is back watching another programme. Zoe is arranging what she needs to take in to *Yiayia*. Marina looks at Bobby, who winks and mouths, 'I'm your man.' Marina smiles. He has kind eyes, but he is a bit of a silly old fool. She closes the door behind her, feeling twenty years younger than when she entered.

Chapter 6

Out on the balcony, it appears the town is still sleepy from the afternoon *mesimeriano* – the siesta. Not many people are stirring yet and few sounds can be heard. Marina feels lighter for her chat with Bobby and heads for the steps, which the cats have now deserted. She begins her ascent at a steady pace and rests every few steps. It is a great deal easier this time and she wonders why she made such a fuss about it earlier.

She stops halfway up and admires the view but decides not to sit down. At the top she will rest, when she reaches the doorstep of the building she once knew. But when she gets there she is invigorated, not tired, and she pushes on, trying to ignore the memories the lonely building evokes. Unwillingly, she is catapulted back through the years and remembers the loneliness she felt then, the months that ticked by. Aunt Efi was kind but Marina wanted to be outside, and she felt scared, constantly.

A little further on, she sees that the shop that was in someone's front room has grown: it occupies three of the whitewashed building's rooms now, and extends into the street. The vegetables on trestle tables are covered with a cloth to show that the shop is closed, but the hessian sacks of rice and beans sit with their tops rolled down, ready for business.

On the left, Marina sees a door she remembers. It is low with no handle and no keyhole, painted a thick, shiny brown. It hasn't changed at all, not even the colour. It was ajar back then too.

Marina snuck out just for a change of scenery, unbelievably bored with being cooped up. She estimated she had an hour or so before Aunt Efi would wake up from her afternoon sleep. She need never know she had been out.

It was the smell that made her curious. A rich smell of honey and something else she couldn't put her finger on. She went closer to the door to breathe in the sweetness more fully. It was dark inside, but through the open crack she could see a flickering light. She pushed the door open slightly. The smell got stronger. The room was dim and it took a minute for Marina's eyes to adjust, and she could see candles hovering. She stepped in, mesmerised by the apparition. The sweet honey aroma, mixed with the smell of wax, was almost overpowering once inside, and she felt pleasantly dizzy.

The room was lit by candles distributed unevenly around the walls, lodged on ledges and in niches between the stones. Years of dripping wax from these crevices had created stalactites and frozen wax rivers that ran to the floor.

The brightest light, though, came from a small fire in a pit in the floor in the middle of the room, over which stood a wide black cauldron full of gently shimmering wax. Marina took all this in but was most intrigued by a ring of metal suspended horizontally over the cauldron. It hung by chains from the rafters and had tails of string evenly spaced around it, the ends dangling just above the molten wax. The white string appeared to glow in the dull light.

The atmosphere was reminiscent of that of a church, and Marina held her breath in awe. She turned to leave when she heard a small soft voice.

'You can help a little, if you like?' Out of the dark shadows a woman appeared, shorter even than Marina. Her grey hair was pinned up at the back of her head in a rather chic French roll, but wisps of hair escaped around her face, which appeared leathery and taut in the candlelight.

Marina mumbled some excuses, but the old lady shuffled forward and whispered, 'Stay,' in a conspiratorial tone. Marina hesitated and turned to look once more at the candles and the pot of shimmering wax, to find the old woman had produced a wooden stool from somewhere, which she patted in invitation. She then turned, before Marina had made her decision, and took, from a wooden peg on the wall, an apron stiff with wax. Pieces flaked off as she moved it, the wax shards disappearing into the well-trodden straw that covered the floor.

Marina edged to the stool and sat cautiously and curiously on its time-worn wooden seat. The old woman continued without looking at her. She bent from the hips and took up a jug that was all but buried in the straw, its edges strangely softened and its contours oddly smooth. Marina was transfixed as the woman dipped the jug into the cauldron of wax and the jug seemed to melt, its contours becoming crisp as the dried wax turned liquid. She used the jug to swirl the lava before lifting it, full of hot wax, to the height of the hanging metal circle. Then she steadily and slowly poured the wax down one of the hanging strings. She turned the metal circle a fraction and poured wax down the next wick, before bending to refill the jug and turning the ring another fraction.

The wicks became infinitesimally thicker as the woman continued to turn the ring and fill and pour the jug. The only sounds were the slow chinking of the chains the ring was supported on as they become twisted with the turning, and the dripping of the wax as it ran down the end of each wick and rejoined the melting pot.

When she had completed the circle she allowed the chains to unwind. Some of the tails of the forming candles caught on each other and she separated them with her fingers before taking a fresh jug of wax and beginning the cycle again.

Marina looked more closely around the room. Behind the cauldron was a wooden table on which stood an unlit oil lamp, a cloth, a flat tin and a cake of something. Behind this, against the wall, were stacked candles a metre or more tall, tapering to a fluff of wick at their tops. Down the side of the walls were rows and rows of open-topped boxes of church candles.

The woman finished another cycle and allowed the ring to spin back again, and when it came to rest she put down the jug, and deliberately and slowly took off her apron. She turned to Marina, looped the apron over her head, picked up the jug and handed it to her, smiling. Marina felt excitement and just a touch of fear. What if she did it wrong, what if the old woman laughed at her attempts? The woman smiled broadly at her hesitation, her paper-thin skin creasing at the corners of her mouth and her cheeks pulled smooth.

Marina paused before dipping the jug and then took courage and began. The old woman took a big flat stick from behind the door and stirred the wax whilst Marina was pouring. Once happy with the consistency, the woman hung the paddle on a hook protruding from the bare stone wall and dragged a wooden box from under the table, from which she took out a wax honeycomb, dark brown, almost black, in the dim light.

Marina positioned herself slightly at an angle to watch what the woman was doing, whilst she continued to pour the wax. Down on the floor in the corner, completely unnoticed until now, Marina could see a pan of boiling water on top of a primitive stove. The woman dropped the wax into the water and returned to the table. She picked up the cake of what Marina now realised must be wax. The bottom of the cake was black. From amongst her skirts she took a knife and began to scrape the black off the cake into the flat tin.

They continued working together like this for some time, the candles growing slowly thicker, until the woman put down the cake of clean wax and went over to the primitive stove. From another hook in the wall she took a sieve and began to scoop the scum off the surface of the pan of simmering water and melted honeycomb. From under the table, with her free hand, she pulled out a newspaper and unfolded it, and onto this she upturned the sieve to tap it clean.

'The cocoons.' She spoke slowly. 'The chickens love them.' She smiled when she had finished speaking. She hung the sieve back on its hook and slowly made her way over to Marina. The woman looked right in her eyes then, and Marina felt such kindness. The woman took the jug and put it on the floor, which relieved Marina as her arm was aching by now with the effort of repeatedly holding it up, full of wax. Then, carefully, gently, the woman lifted the apron over Marina's head and replaced it around her own neck. She picked up the jug and began her work again.

Marina took one last look around the room before slipping out of the door into blinding sunshine, as quietly as she had entered. Her last thought was to wonder how the woman got in when there was no door handle or keyhole.

She runs her hand across the door as she passes, the memory precious. She only met that kind woman on one other occasion.

Marina inhales deeply to bring herself back into the present. She turns right onto a path of large, flat flagstones. Further up, the stone path gives way to a rough, narrow, cobbled lane between the whitewashed houses. Cats sprawl on doorsteps here and there. Some doors are open, revealing dark sitting rooms or steps straight up to the first floor or, in the grander houses, courtyards large and small.

Eventually the cobbles give way to bare earth, with stones sticking through where the winter rain has washed the soil from around them. Baked rivulets of brown mud surround islands of pebbles. The larger stones have creases of earth piled above them and trailing wakes of disturbed soil below, all scorched beneath the Mediterranean sun to a hard dry path.

The pine trees are close, their shade beckoning, beyond the last of the houses. The path now twists and turns on itself, down three steps to go up six, under an arch between two buildings, round the corner, too narrow for more than one person at a time. Round the next corner is the unexpected pleasure of encountering an old woman in black, sitting on a doorstep, happy to wish Marina a good walk. A donkey to pass, some cats to stroke, some geese in someone's garden.

The houses thin out and give way to rough ground, but Marina has remembered the path and, as it advances onto open ground – too high to build, too rocky to grow things – it suddenly becomes cobbles again and then flags, and finally she is under the shade of the pine trees.

She is impressed with how well she is doing. The island is steep but the path smooth, and Marina begins to wonder what she will say to Yanni, or his mother. It is hard to imagine Yanni as a cute baby, and Marina conjures up an image of a baby with a scowl. Maybe his mother scowls too? How could a mother scowl at her child? Marina takes a deep breath. She wipes a tear away. She should have loved him more. How was she to know?

When you are just married to someone you don't really like, and you are only fifteen, you want to escape. It is only natural, she tells herself. Well, she escaped by playing with her friends. She would forget everything for hours at a time. She was a young fifteen and she loved to play hopscotch, tag, and a game called poison, using a length of rope. Her friends ranged from four-year-olds to sixteen-year-old girls, the boys being away on the farms by that age.

The baby came very soon after they were married. It made hopscotch difficult near the end of her time. The baby was just beautiful. A boy. She called him Dimitri, but Manolis said he should be named after his grandfather, Socrates. But no baby has an official name until it is baptised in the Greek Orthodox Church. So it was just 'baby' at first.

Marina's mother helped with the baby right from the start, and as the days passed she helped more and more, until she took over altogether. Her mum understood Marina's need to be with her peers. The baby cried a lot and would never settle down. Marina would play outside as much as she could, avoiding her domestic responsibilities. She loved her baby, but once she was outside she would forget she even had a son. It's hard when you are fifteen – your mind's not ready. She thought about today's fifteen-year-olds. Girls that age don't play hopscotch these days, they play video games and dress like pop stars. But that was then. She was young for her age and there were no video games or pop stars.

Her mother would call her in when he needed feeding and Marina would coo and cluck like any other mother. She would spend time playing with him and making him laugh, but after a while she felt cooped up and wanted to be out playing again, and besides, he looked like Manolis, which didn't help.

But if she had known, she would have loved him more. Her mother said she had expected it, that he was a weak thing from the start. Marina felt it was her fault. If she had loved him more, if she had fed him more... Her mother tried to calm her, and insisted there was nothing she could have done; sometimes that's just how life is.

Manolis was quiet when he was in the house for a while after that, and he didn't come near Marina, which suited her very well. She moved into the second bedroom and stayed there. Six years later

Eleni was born, the product of a drunken night for Manolis. Artemis, five years after Eleni, was the result of a drunken night for Marina who desperately wanted another child.

With all her thoughts crowding in on her, Marina suddenly realises she has reached the top and the pine forest is petering out. An unexpected sign tells her that the monastery is to her right, and the ridge at the top of the island to her left.

Chapter 7

Marina sits on the flat-topped rock she has claimed as her picnic chair and brushes the cheese-pie crumbs from her blouse. She holds her arms out to the side to allow her underarms to dry in the breeze. She feels somewhat revived by the food but really needs a good meal. That will have to wait. She adjusts her feet and stands. She is tired, but at least going back will be all downhill. Then again, there is no point in being up here at all unless she talks to Yanni, or his parents, and besides, she really needs a drink of water.

She pushes past the last of the trees and the ridge opens out before her. A couple of cypress trees stretch to the blue sky a short distance away, with bushes at their feet, indicating the presence of people – it is unlikely that they would have self-seeded and stayed alive up here without some nurturing in their early years. Through the bushes there is a hint of orange. Marina wonders if it is a tiled roof. As she gets closer she can see it is a single-storey shepherd's cottage. Marina runs her hand across the whitewashed stone, large boulders at the base supporting smaller and smaller stones towards the roof. Layers of thick whitewash defuse the contours, softening the whole into an organic mound.

Goat bells can be heard behind the building and Marina rounds the windowless dwelling, past the bushes, to see two donkeys munching placidly from their nosebags. A little distance away a woman sits on a barrel, and in the hammock of her skirt stands a tiny kid that she is bottle-feeding. It sucks hungrily, pushing vigorously at the bottle, and the woman's stout arms brace in resistance. Her free hand helps the kid keep its balance, its little hooves tap-dancing in excitement, the woman's skirt being tested for strength.

'Hello, how are things?' Marina, up here so far from anything, leaves ceremony behind.

'*Kalimera!* Come help me feed the goat!' The woman, not startled, beams happily and greets Marina as if she has known her all her life. There is no space for formality in these surroundings. It is a survival existence, everyone pulls together.

'I think I am thirstier than your goats!' Marina sits on a box next to the lady and takes the bottle and the baby goat, which bleats furiously at the interruption to its meal. The lady disappears into the dark of the hut. Marina puts her arm around the kid to stop it falling off her knee. The goat's odour is pungent and not unpleasant. The woman reappears with a tin mug and a bottle of water, which she puts on the ground next to Marina, who is now struggling with the kid as it thrusts at the bottle, its spiky little hooves bruising her thighs.

The bottle empties and the baby goat pushes and noses with even greater energy, its upright tail wagging backwards and forwards at a frantic pace. Marina pulls the bottle from its reluctant mouth to stop the little mite gulping air. It bleats in protest. Marina lowers it to the ground and it skips and jumps about until the woman lifts it into a square pen with three other kids. They happily headbutt each other.

'Done!' she announces, and slaps both thighs as she sits back on her barrel.

Marina is on her second mug of water.

'So, are you out for a walk?'

Marina finishes drinking and wipes her mouth on the back of her hand.

'Yes, I felt the need to be away from people.'

'Naturally! I spend the winter months down there.' The woman jerks her thumb towards the path down to the main town. 'That's enough for me. Trouble is, when I come up here my husband and son follow. There's no peace!' She chuckles.

'Now, how would they be surviving without you?'

'Exactly! But I tell Yanni, my son, he should stay down in the summer. He won't get any trade up here.' As if on cue, one of the donkeys bursts into a yodelling bray, drawing its call out at the end, thinning to nothing. The sound echoes down the hill.

A man strides from the hut, tucking in his shirt.

'Hello,' Marina says. It takes her a minute to recognise him as Yanni from the port, with his hair all over his face.

'Eh?' He pushes his hair back and walks to one of the donkeys and strokes its nose, before striding over to the wooden saddles behind them and lifting one onto the larger donkey's back.

'Well, he can have a little trade now if he's going back down. I am exhausted. What do you say, Yanni? Give an old woman a lift down the hill?' Marina giggles.

'Sure he will!' A man hobbles out of the hut, pulling up his braces. 'He's a good lad, a bit moody, but good to his mother and me. Are you not, Yanni?'

'*Nai, Baba.*' Yes, Dad. He saddles the second donkey and makes to leave. Marina sees an opportunity to ask him a few questions along the way if she accompanies him, but shies from his gruff attitude. She hopes it is not him that she is looking for.

He walks towards the path, leading the first donkey, the second roped behind.

'Yanni, give the lady a ride?' The woman stands up from her barrel and puts a friendly hand on Marina's shoulder.

'I'll walk with you a little first, and when I can walk no more I'll hop on!' Marina addresses Yanni, and finds the mental picture of herself hopping onto a donkey amusing and giggles. Yanni sees no humour in the situation.

'As you like.' He doesn't look at her as he replies.

'Goodbye, then. Thank you for the water.' Marina shakes the woman's hand.

'Thank you for feeding the goat. Come again next time the people are too much!' The woman slaps her heartily on the shoulder.

'Yanni, get me some razors, I look like a wild man,' his father calls.

They set off on the path along the ridge, heading down towards the pine forest, Yanni on one side of the lead donkey, Marina on the other, the haunches of the donkeys dipping and rising as they find their feet down the rocky slope. Marina is thankful she has worn her old shoes again. They make slow progress at first, down the top slope of the ridge.

Marina tries to think of the most subtle way to phrase the questions she wants to ask. 'Very remote up here.' She wishes she hadn't said that, it's too vague. Yanni does not reply.

'How long have you lived up here in the summer?' Better.

'All my life.' He keeps his eyes on the path.

'Even when you were a boy?' Marina wishes she was naturally sly.

'All my life.' He twists his moustache with his fingers.

'Surely as a boy you preferred to be with other boys down in the town, playing football and so on?' Marina thinks this is a good question.

'No.'

'What about as a baby? Perhaps it was a bit hot up there in the summer for you as a baby?' Marina turns her face away to hide her embarrassment, aware of what a ridiculous question this is. When she turns back, Yanni gives her a look of contempt but does not reply. Marina cannot think of anything else to say. Yanni offers nothing. He moves his hand further up the rope he is leading the donkey by.

'And surely your *yiayia* would not be happy with you being so far from her. She was in the town?' Marina's cheeks colour. It does not come naturally to her to pry.

Yanni takes a single cigarette out of his shirt pocket and lights it with a lighter from his jeans. He takes a long drag before putting the lighter away. Marina waits, feeling sure he is about to say something.

'*Yiayia* Sophia was up there until she died. She was born up there. Born and died there. I will do the same.' He flicks the loose end of the rope at the donkey to make it walk faster.

'Ah. No girlfriends beckoning you into the town then?' Yanni casts a sour look and clicks his disdain with his tongue on the roof of his mouth, an emphatic Greek 'No'.

'You ride now.' It is not a question. Yanni has stopped the donkeys and adjusts the saddle on the rear animal before beckoning Marina round. He offers his hands, fingers locked together, as a step-up. Marina pulls hard on the donkey's saddle and Yanni hoists her up as if she weighs nothing. She sits traditionally, side-saddle.

'My, you are strong,' Marina chuckles. Yanni, grim-faced, pulls the saddle straight before he returns to the lead animal and takes up the rope rein. He gives it length, using it like a leash, seemingly to create as much distance as he can from Marina. She understands the message and doesn't mind. She has the information she wants, and she is very happy he is not with Eleni – or anyone else, for that matter! Let him be grumpy, she will focus on her beautiful surroundings. They have an hour – less, maybe – before sunset, and the island is peaceful.

They enter the pine forest and the sounds of the hooves are muffled, everything else silent. Marina enjoys the sway of the motion and looks up at the hues of the pale-blue sky through the treetops, towards the town, until under the tree branches, down by the water, the sky glows softly pink and orange as the sun drops into the sea.

Marina thinks she may have even drifted off a little with the gentle sway of her mild animal. The journey down seems even quicker than she expected. As they leave the pine trees Marina realises that Yanni might be going down to the right, to the area Zoe had pointed out as being the vicinity of the store that kept her order. A more direct route back for Marina will be to the left.

'Hey?' she calls.

Yanni stops the train and turns his head, an unlit cigarette dangling under his moustache, lighter poised.

'I'll jump down here and go left, quicker for me.'

'As you wish.' He offers her no assistance for her descent, so Marina just slides, a very dignified dismount. She smiles at her ability.

'OK, how much do I owe you?' Marina scrabbles in her bag for her purse as she walks towards him.

'Nothing.' He is looking down at the port.

'But I must, it is work.'

'I was coming down anyway.' He takes up the reins, holding them close in to the donkey's mouth.

'I insist.'

'Insist all you like.' He clicks with his tongue to signal the animals on and begins his steady walk, away to the right. Marina finds a two-euro piece and runs to catch him up. He falters, and she tucks the two euros in his chest pocket.

'Buy yourself a coffee.' Marina smiles.

'As you like.' He twists his moustache and clicks the donkeys on.

Marina smiles again as he walks away.

The way through the houses back to Zoe's is a joy after such an easy descent, each house a step nearer to a prolonged rest. The cheese pie she ate is a distant memory and her stomach rumbles. At a corner, a sign above a stone arch announces the *Taverna tou Kapetaniou*. There is no need to make a choice, the 'Captain's Restaurant' will do fine, and Marina marches in.

The courtyard is a cool haven, with vines growing up three walls and across a wooden frame, providing a ceiling of leaves. Crude paintings hang on the walls and in the corner a boy is picking through a piece he

84

is learning from sheet music on his bouzouki. They are alone except for a couple in the corner, obviously English, or maybe Dutch, by their 'everything-new-but-slightly-scruffy' look, Marina decides. Marina has had years of practice in guessing the nationalities of lost tourists coming into her shop. She smiles at them. It is too early for most diners.

The waiter takes his time and eventually ambles over to her table. He wishes her a good evening and begins to list all the food that is ready, or can be prepared quickly, in the kitchen.

Marina orders a large Greek salad of cucumber and tomatoes, stuffed vine leaves and *saganaki* – she just loves this grilled cheese, even though she suspects it is not good for her, but, after all, she has walked a very long way today. She wonders if the stuffed vines leaves will be from a tin. When they come they are fresh and obviously home-made. Marina doesn't even need to squeeze lemon over them as they are served in a light lemon sauce, into which she delights in dipping her bread. She has just begun when she decides to be daring. She catches the waiter's eye and orders a quarter of a kilo of red wine. She feels like a queen, presiding over her table for one, and doesn't stop eating until she feels she might burst.

The bouzouki boy is making progress with his piece until his mother comes out and orders him inside to do his homework. The resulting quiet silences the gentle talk of the English couple – Marina has decided they are English after all – who, after a pause, begin to converse again in hushed whispers.

Marina pushes her chair away from the table and leans back. No sooner has she has done this than a black-and-white cat jumps on her knee, demanding attention. Full and happy, Marina strokes the cat and feeds it leftovers. It turns its nose up at the salad but is keen on everything else. Marina finishes the wine and takes a piece of paper from her bag. It is her list of one to twenty with *Yanni – donkey man* written against number one. She looks in her bag and finds a pencil. Licking the end of the pencil, she flattens the sheet on the table and puts a line through his name with great satisfaction, and a big cross at the end of it. One down.

The remaining numbers stare emptily back at her. *It will come.* Marina feels, at this moment, with half a carafe of wine and a good meal inside her, that she can do anything.

The English couple pay and leave, and the restaurant begins to fill. Greek families with young children and American tourists, mostly, and a few Germans, Dutch, and a Japanese couple whom Marina thinks she vaguely recognises from earlier that day. She begins to feel sleepy. With the long hours in her shop she always needs to catch up on her sleep. She pays her bill and leaves a generous tip. She was grateful for the fresh food and passes her thanks on to the chef. The waiter tells her to wait a second, the chef is his father, and he comes out to shake her hand. He is flattered by her compliments and they chat about serving the public and the decline of tourism. He suggests she comes again and says, 'We will not charge you tourist prices!' Marina forgets to ask the waiter how old he is and doesn't remember until she has left, when she decides it is too late, and besides, she is sure she is a little drunk...

She walks slowly back to Zoe's. She climbs the stairs and is passing Zoe's door on the way to her own room when she hears her name called. She is too tired to answer but the call comes again. It is not Zoe calling, the words are too slurred. One more time, and she realises it is Roula. She pushes the door open.

'Everything all right, Roula?' she asks. There is no sign of Zoe.

'Shh, Mum is sleeping,' Roula whispers.

'Sorry.' Marina backs out of the door.

'Wait! Mrs Marina,' Roula hisses.

Marina opens the door again and Roula hands her a piece of paper. She hears a guttural chuckle. Bobby is slumped lower than usual in his chair and his head is nodding to his laugh.

Marina opens the sheet and finds a list of names.

'What's this?' Marina asks.

'It's what you asked for. I told you I was your man.' Bobby's jacket has all but fallen off, and as he laughs he slips further in his chair.

'Shh!' Roula commands.

Marina slides into the room and straightens his jacket and offers to pull him up a bit. He accepts without embarrassment. She hears him drawing in her scent as she lifts him into his chair. The old scoundrel.

'Where did you get this?' she whispers, holding the list in front of him.

'Aha, that would be telling.' Bobby's eyes shine.

'From me,' Roula hisses. She is watching the television with the sound off.

'How would you–?'

'*Yiayia* told me.' She is bouncing a little, excited by the event, but still with her eyes on the screen.

Bobby chuckles to himself, proud of his teasing ways that got Roula to engage *Yiayia* enough to recall the good old days, and to translate whilst he wrote it all down. Holding the pen and paper was the biggest challenge. He stops chuckling and looks at his gnarled twisted hands. 'These bloody hands!' he says out loud.

'Uncle Bobby, that's rude!' Roula hisses.

'Shh, Roula. You'll wake your mum.' Bobby is teasing.

'So how does *Yiayia* know all the boys aged thirty-five that are still on the island?' Marina asks.

'She was a teacher back in those days. Once she worked out one name of someone who must be thirty-five this year, that was it! The whole class came back to her, and some of the nicknames too. I haven't heard her laugh so much ever. Really cheered her up.'

Marina is beaming. 'So this is all the boys?'

'Well, no, we took off the names of those we knew had died – that was three of the poor buggers.' Bobby's eyes take on a sorrowful look.

'Uncle Bobby! Bugger's rude!'

'Shh, Roula. You'll wake Zoe.' He grins at her and she turns to stick her tongue out at him. 'Then, I knew two of the names of families that have moved away, ones that were friends of Zoe's. So you are left with a list of possibilities, who may or may not be here.'

'Well, Bobby, you are a sly one! Thank you, Roula.' Marina can see Roula is back in her own television world.

'What?' Roula says.

'Thank you for helping,' Marina replies.

'Helping with what?' She is absorbed in the wordless screen.

'Never mind. Bobby, where is *Yiayia*, so I can thank her?'

'She is sleeping now, but she will not remember a word of what we have talked about. Give it a few days and neither will Roula. In fact, your only threat will be me. So you had better be nice to me. If I was a young man again…'

'Shh.' Bobby's voice is rising now.

'It's OK, Roula, I am going now anyway. Thank you very much.' Marina waves the paper.

'Good luck.' Bobby tries to wave a twisted hand in response.

Marina steps outside the door and hears Bobby whisper 'Keep me informed' before the door closes completely.

Tired as she is, she nearly skips her way back to her room, where she opens the window wide, kicks her shoes off and lies face down on the bed to read her list. There are fewer names than she expected and it takes a little moment to understand the shaky writing.

Costas Voulgaris – The Cockerel – because he was noisy – Father owned kafeneio by the port.

Panayotis (Panos) – His father was a barber. Yiayia has seen young Panos walking past the house.

Socrates Rappas – Always fiddling with things, quiet.

Yannis Harimis – Known as 'Black Yanni' because he is so brown in the summer – his Yiayia was the midwife.

Aris Kranidiotis – Very naughty – his sister married the papas from the church across on the mainland.

Apostolis (Tolis) Kaloyannis – His father owned the boatyard on the mountain village path.

Alexandros Mavromatis – She says he made her laugh. Known as 'The Butterfly' for his flitting from one girl to the next.

Marina can picture them all sitting in class. Most of them would probably have left before they were twelve, and it's unlikely they would have attended regularly during their time at school. It occurs to Marina that the person she is looking for might never even have been to school. They might not have come down from the mountain village. She dismisses the thought as it makes things too complicated.

Taking out her pencil, she enjoys putting a line through Yanni for a second time, although he was very kind about not wanting payment for taking her down the hill on his donkey, and his mother was lovely. She releases the pressure as she finishes drawing the line, relenting her harsh opinion. His *yiayia* was the midwife. She puts a full stop at the end of the line.

Marina hears a mosquito, and slips her feet half back in her shoes to turn out the light and open the window wider, hoping the irritating creature will fly out seeking somewhere lighter. She pauses to look over the town below the ridge at night. It is so beautiful, the whitewashed houses now blue-grey with eyes of orange. She goes out onto the front balcony where she can see out to the sea. On the paths between the houses lights are dotted brightly at uneven intervals and warm interior lights glow in between them where shutters are still open. The moon is bright and the whitewashed walls appear ghostly, but the warmth in the air and the smell of jasmine nearby give the view a romance that stirs Marina's soul. She can hear the muted tones of a bouzouki coming from a far corner, and quite unexpectedly a donkey brays, his retching sound echoing from across the gully where houses descend to the harbour.

Someone shouts from another quarter at the donkey to be quiet.

Chapter 8

The next day Marina finds herself in the harbour early. There is a welcome breeze, cooling everything down. The port is like an ants' nest, a mass of people all busy doing something or going somewhere. There is a large ship at the pier. Marina came down to buy breakfast from the bakery but decides to sit at one of the cafés and watch life a little. After some time the waiter stops chatting to his friend and ambles up to her.

'*Nai*?' He has no notebook for her order, and his white shirt is a little grey.

'Ah yes, frappé, sweet, and do you have any *bougatza*?' Marina tries not to eat *bougatza* too often. The soft pastry with cream filling is delicious but does nothing to help her clothes fit her.

'*Nai*.' He flashes the most charming smile at her and Marina feels like a tourist. It is quite exciting. She smooths her blouse and sits up a little straighter. His trousers fit well.

'What's the big boat?' Marina asks just as he pivots to leave.

'*Zeus*. Three islands, one-day tour. Drops the tourists off for an hour, they spend their money, take pictures, and leave.' He bends to stroke a cat before taking her order indoors.

Further along the quayside, a pair of donkeys are being loaded; on the front one is luggage, and on the rear one a Japanese tourist: a woman in white gloves, holding a parasol. Marina wonders why they wear white gloves. If it is to protect them from dirt then surely black ones would be more practical – less washing to do whilst they are away from home.

The donkeys wind their way through the throng, and to Marina's surprise Yanni says hello as he passes her, and she smiles and waves.

She sits for a while and enjoys people-watching, and her coffee. The breeze is getting stronger. There is a yacht trying to leave the harbour. It reverses and she can hear the rattling of the anchor chain as it is winched in. The man leaning over the bows, watching the chain, puts up his hand to signal to the man at the helm. He shouts something – in German, Marina guesses. The boat moves forward again, letting out its chain, and then tries again, but still the anchor is stuck. The German crew line the rail of the yacht, leaning over to look into the water, and all talk at once. The yacht swings helplessly on its mooring, stuck fast, the anchor presumably snagged on something on the sea bed.

A burly man on the dock hails them. He strips off his shirt and mimics diving. The helmsman nods acceptance with a relieved look on his face, and the burly man, who has a very hairy chest, dives into the water, swims like a fish to the bows of the yacht, takes a deep breath and disappears.

Marina calls the waiter for the bill, then stands to leave as she waits for her change. As the waiter counts out coins she sees the burly hairy man appear again on the surface. He shouts to the helmsman, who fishes in his pocket, unfolds some bills and throws them to the man in the water. He catches the floating notes, rolls them up and puts them in his mouth like a cigarette before heading back to the shore.

'I don't suppose you know a barber called Panos, do you?' Marina asks the waiter.

'Panos, *nai*,' he answers in the affirmative.

'Does he have a shop?' The waiter explains how to find the shop and flashes another sparkling smile. Marina's movements become more feminine as she walks away. She allows her hips to wiggle ever so slightly.

She turns for a last glimpse back. The yacht is now taking in its anchor easily and the hairy man is putting his shirt back on. The waiter has disappeared.

Marina walks across the harbour to the corner where the commercial boats tie up. At this point she turns right on the wide path inland.

The lane is lined, for a short distance, with stalls selling lace. Large pieces hang from coat hangers strung on string, stretched from rusty nails across the shopfronts. Smaller pieces are draped over the tiny shops' shutters. There are pieces on trays on the ground and women sit on stools in the shop doorways tatting new pieces, their fingers dancing spiders spinning their creations.

Marina, as instructed, passes the lacemakers and turns hard left. The lane is very narrow, single file only, and she wonders if she has taken a wrong turn as the way ahead, further along, is blocked by a wall. But she sees, as she draws level with it, a recessed door frame that has been painted in red and white diagonal stripes. There is no door. An arrow painted on the wall inside the door frame points up the stairs, which to Marina seems funny as there is no other way to go. She smiles to herself. The steps have dropped slightly so Marina feels that with each tread she could slide backwards. They are thickly painted in grey and the middle of each has been worn smooth, back to the wood. She holds the handrail, which rattles on loose screws. At the top of the steps another door stands open to a room from which light pours, from floor-to-ceiling windows that overlook the port. The panes are not large and several have cracks running across them. Two, near the bottom, have been boarded up. But the view through them is magnificent, the mismatched cracked windows giving the impression of a stained-glass replica of the harbour scene.

There is a strip of mirror, also floor to ceiling, on one wall by the window, reflecting even more light into the room, and through this Marina first sees the man's back. Tall, with neat hair – *well he would, wouldn't he?* – wide shoulders, narrow hips, perfectly

96

proportioned. 'Smart but casual', Marina thinks the term is. Perfect. She gazes at him with compassionate eyes. He is sweeping the unadorned wooden floor around a single barber's chair.

Marina turns away from the mirror to face him in the flesh; she blushes slightly, and her movements become awkward.

'Welcome.' The man smiles. He has beautiful teeth, and holds out his hand. Marina breaks her gaze and shakes it. 'What can I do for you?' he asks.

Marina hesitates. She has not prepared for this moment, and it suddenly feels as if it has all happened rather too quickly for her to gather her thoughts. If this is Eleni's young man – *and let's be honest, what young lady would not want him as her young man?* – he is bound to tell Eleni that she has been asking questions and, even if those questions lead nowhere, Eleni will still be furious. Marina feels she cannot think fast enough.

'Pano?' she asks. The man nods, so she continues. 'I have a son.' Marina looks at the floor and then furtively at Panos, afraid the lies will show. 'He is not on this island.' She doesn't want to start by giving the man competition. 'He is thinking of opening a barbershop.' She impresses herself with her quick thinking.

Panos indicates the chair and Marina sits. Panos produces some glasses and pours them both some water from a plastic bottle. It is already hot in his shop – more of a greenhouse than a shop, with all those windows. Marina conjures an image of herself

97

as a flower with petals around her head and chuckles. Panos looks at her enquiringly and she thanks him for the water.

His smile broadens into a grin. He has a boyish look about him, despite the thin layer of stubble. 'Oh yes. A good trade, men always want their hair cutting, and when they don't their wives want them to have it cut anyway,' he informs her, and as he laughs he wraps his arms across his thin, tight T-shirt, his muscles bulging, veins prominent. Thin skin, thinks Marina, I bet he scars easily, poor boy.

She pulls herself back to the moment. 'Do you think an island is a good place to start or would he be better off on the mainland?'

Panos unwraps his arms and pulls a stool from against the wall, his limbs supple, his movements like liquid. 'An island is a captured clientele, they have no choice! But the mainland has more people, so it is probably the same.'

'Do you think,' Marina selects each word carefully, her speech slowing, 'that being born and raised on an island, with a local family, makes it easier?'

'Oh yes. My father was a barber before me, which helped to bring the old boys in, but I went to school with the majority of my clients.' Panos really does have amazing teeth, so white. The whites of his eyes are very white too.

Marina feels she is doing quite well and relaxes. 'Yes, that would help, wouldn't it? Do you think you got your skills from your dad?'

'That's what he says.' Panos laughs and wraps his arms around himself again and leans back against the wall. 'Mum says the old boys come in because I am the spitting image of her – she was a bit of a looker in her day, bless her.'

Panos looks at the floor and shakes his head. 'I moved from the island to Athens for a while. I found the island too – how shall I put it? – limiting, for someone like me, for a while.'

Marina feels she has lost the thread of the conversation somewhere and begins to frown. Panos catches the frown and shifts in his seat. At that moment, footsteps can be heard on the steps, then a young woman enters the room. Panos stands. Marina is immediately on the alert for signs that this is his girlfriend.

'Hello,' the woman says. Nice face, but doesn't match Panos. She is wearing pale-grey linen trousers with a white shirt over the top. She looks cool in the heat; her clothes are for comfort and her hair is tied in a loose knot by itself. Marina guesses it must be very long to be able to do that and thinks of the work it must take to wash and dry.

Panos fills her in on Marina's enquiry and the girl nods knowingly. There is something very calming about her, and Marina immediately likes her. Her voice is soothing and her movements graceful, no rush. She also looks very strong. Marina searches for the words to describe her. Sinewy! Practical. Yes, not one to avoid work for breaking a nail. She giggles and then coughs to cover it and says, 'Hello, you must be Panos's girlfriend? Or his wife?'

Both the girl and Panos now laugh, but when they see Marina is not joining in they pull themselves together and Panos opens his mouth to speak. Apparently, their brief laughter has covered the sound of more footsteps on the stairs as a young man with golden hair unexpectedly strides into the room. Just as Panos is about to speak, and before the blonde man sees Marina, he ruffles the girl's hair and leans across her to give Panos a lingering kiss on the lips. Marina cannot help her audible intake of breath.

The golden-haired man starts, Panos blushes and the girl smiles serenely.

'And here we have the reason I found the island difficult for a while and why I moved to Athens briefly…' Panos grins at Marina. The blonde man says hello.

Marina isn't as taken aback as she thought she would be. Of course, she has read about such things and there is always gossip about one person or the other in the village, and the usual teasing of the weaker boys growing up. But here are two men, neither of them weak, both – well, to be honest, very handsome, and they are – what would you call them? – a couple. Marina feels strangely liberated. *Why not?* She smiles warmly at the new man, and returns his hello.

The young people relax as they see that Marina is neither shocked nor embarrassed. They all smile warmly back at her. Marina considers how she must look to them. Her hair is greying a little, her skin is sun-worn, she is dressed in black and she is a little stout. To them she must look like a regular old woman. She doubts they expect a positive response from someone like her. She smiles, thinking of herself as a cool old lady, and then chastises herself for calling herself old, when she's not even fifty yet.

Marina stands and thanks them for their time. She can, obviously, cross this young man off the list of possibles as Eleni's boyfriend. A shame, because she liked him, and his friends. They tell her to drop by any time if she wants to 'hang out'. Her initial response is to check her blouse is tucked in, but fortunately this is misconstrued as a joke and makes them smile all the more, and they encourage her to return.

She is about to leave but takes one last look out of the magnificent window and sees that *Zeus* has gone. In its place a hydrofoil is tying up and the passengers are getting off. An old couple are struggling with the steps down from the vessel, and behind them is a girl who looks remarkably like Eleni.

'Panayia!' Marina exclaims to her god, and she can feel the blood drain from her face.

The three friends turn to look out of the window to see what has caused their new friend such consternation, but they do not detect anything out of the ordinary. When they turn back to Marina she has gone, her feet slipping on the steps. She makes it down the last two on her bottom.

The lace shops have taken in a great deal of their wares now the tourist boat has gone; there is more room to move but there are fewer places to hide. The lace left hanging is banging against the shutters as the wind has really picked up now.

Thoughts race through Marina's mind. Is Eleni here permanently? Has she moved early or has she just come for a day or two? She was not supposed to be starting work for another three months or so. Marina feels exposed and wants to return to her room to think things through. But that means passing through the open port area. She edges towards the harbour and scans the faces for Eleni. She cannot see her at first, but then spots her bending over, zipping up her case before standing to walk on, less than ten metres away. Marina tries to think. She could go up the lane she is on, inland, and try to find her way across town in the back streets, but she would probably get lost, or… There is no 'or'.

Marina has spent too long thinking. Eleni begins to straighten right in front of her. Marina ducks into the nearest lace shop and grabs a piece of lace, which she holds up to the light on pretence of inspecting the detail, neatly obscuring her face. She can see Eleni though the holes. Eleni is walking slowly and searching her pocket for something. She evidently finds what she is looking for and she holds it in front of her and fiddles. It is her mobile phone.

'She will be calling her lover to say she is here,' Marina tells the lace.

'Pardon?' asks a little old lady behind the counter.

102

Marina hadn't noticed the woman put down the lace she was making on her stool and come inside.

'Beautiful work,' Marina exclaims, and, hitching her handbag further up her arm, she exchanges the piece of lace she is holding for another with bigger holes. Eleni has stopped walking and is standing outside the shop with her phone to her ear.

Marina hopes she will speak his name, and she moves towards the door with her lace disguise to eavesdrop.

A noise from Marina's handbag startles her and she tells it to hush, hugging her bag to her chest with the lace over it, and retreating to the furthest corner of the shop with her back to the door. She scrabbles in her bag. The noise is coming from the mobile phone Artemis gave her. 'For emergencies, Mum. You never know.'

She looks at the phone blankly. The little old lady watches her.

'I don't know how to answer it! I never use it,' she whispers to the widow clad in black. She feels sure that Eleni will have heard the noise and will spot her at any moment. Damn the noise it is making.

The old lady leans over and presses a button with a little green phone on it and says, 'Talk.'

Marina puts the phone to her ear and tentatively answers, 'Hello?'

'Mum? Mum, why are you whispering?'

'Eleni?' she turns to the door where Eleni is still standing, phone to her ear, with her back to Marina.

'Mum, can you hear me? I have given notice on my flat in Piraeus but I have to wait till the first of the month to move into the place on the island. They've given me a week off for the move so I'm coming home for a couple of days.'

Marina turns and stares at the back of Eleni's head. Her eyes widen.

'But you said you weren't moving for three months!'

'They've brought it forward. I have to go, I'll see you tomorrow.'

Marina turns, her mouth hanging slightly open, and watches Eleni pocket her phone and walk off up the lane, inland.

'You finished talking?' the old lady asks. Marina nods, and the old lady reaches across and presses a red button on the phone.

'That will be five euros,' she says.

'For what?' Marina asks, looking at her phone. The widow points to the scrunched piece of lace Marina has been balling in her free hand. Marina is surprised to see it there. She apologises for the lace and thanks the woman for her help at the same time, fishing in her bag to pay, then hurries from the shop down to the harbour front.

The donkey man she met when she first arrived waves to her cheerfully. The hair he pulls across his bald head is whipping about in all directions in the wind. She hurries past, distracted, to the nearest taxi boat.

'Aha! It is the lady who owes me a Greek dance halfway across the water. Hello, hello again.' He offers his hand to shake, whereupon he takes hers and puts it to his lips and kisses it. Marina thinks this is a bit smooth but smiles, even though she is in a hurry.

'Please can you take me to the little harbour and then across to the mainland?'

'For you, pretty lady...' he begins, but she has already jumped on board. He stands looking down at her.

'Come on. Come on.' Marina feels flustered. She has to get home before Eleni, or Costas might happily tell her she is on the island and then there would be explaining to do. The threads she is hanging on by are so tentative. She wipes away a tear at the thought.

'But lady...'

'Please just take me to the little harbour. I am in a hurry.'

The man seems very relaxed and amused. 'I can take you to the little...' The roar of the engine drowns the rest of his sentence. He is smiling as he talks, and smoothing his hair back with his free hand.

The little boat neatly backs out between the ever increasing (it seems to Marina) tally of yachts and boats. He swings the vessel round in the mouth of the inlet and powers off to the little harbour. The water seems very choppy, and a quantity of it makes its way inside the boat.

The journey is not long. Marina is already on her feet before the rocking has ceased and clambers up the steps before the man has risen from his bouncy bucket seat. She leaps with more agility than she expects onto shore and shouts 'Wait!' to the captain, who smiles and salutes.

Marina walks as briskly as she can to Zoe's. She pulls her holdall from under the bed, makes a last check around the room and closes the door behind her.

Zoe is glad of the cash and delighted that Marina says she will be returning in a few days. Bobby keeps trying to attract her attention, mouthing 'What is going on?', but Marina leaves before she can form a reply.

Going back to the little harbour is easy, the gentle slope in her favour. With a sigh of relief she sees the taxi boat is still waiting.

'Thank you for waiting. To the mainland, let's go!' Marina steps into the rocking craft.

'Lady, I would love to take you, but as I said there is an *apagoreftiko*!'

'What? What do you mean? I need to go across! What's an *apagoreftiko*?'

'Ah, you see, the wind. It has grown too strong. The port police, they say it is dangerously strong and they forbid all boats to leave the port. I can take you from the little port to the main port but I cannot take you out across open water. No one can leave. It is not allowed, it is an *apagoreftiko*.'

Marina's adrenaline fever dissipates. She blows air through buzzing lips, deflating like a balloon. She rolls her weight forward and allows the man to help her onto the dock. She looks down into the clear water. She can see the bottom; she can see down to little fish swimming in the shade cast by the blue-and-white boat. On the surface is a reflection of colours, unbroken on the harbour's still water, the vessel's hull clean and clear in its mirror image. The rope the man is holding sinks in an arch into the water and out again to the boat, tiny ripples around where it breaks the water's surface.

'Hey, lady, you look sad. Do you dislike the island so much?' There is a bench by the edge of the harbour and he sits on it, still holding the rope. He pats the bench next to him in invitation. Marina accepts and sits down.

'Do you have children?' She feels defeated.

The man's head rolls back with a loud 'Hah!' It sounds slightly bitter.

'Lady, I have just found the right girl for me, just as the world is going crazy. We would love to get married and have children but we have no steady future. The world is an unsure place for young people today.'

'What about your boat?' It occurs to Marina that, if she cannot leave, neither can Eleni, and this gives her hope.

'The owner, a friend of mine, will be back for it at the end of the year and then…'

'And then?' Marina asks. Eleni might catch the first boat in the morning, and then a bus. If Marina takes a taxi boat at first light and drives directly she is sure to get home before her. She begins to relax, enjoying the sheltered corner they have found.

'And then, who knows, we may have to leave the island. Go to Athens, but what would I do there?'

'Where are your parents?'

'They live on the hill behind us.' He gestures with his thumb. 'They are farmers.'

'Can you not work with them? You will inherit the farm?' Marina wonders how early she should set out in the morning.

'The farm is leased, they do not own it. When they die the lease will expire. It is only small, enough for them, but it is not a future for me.'

'That's a shame.' She feels for the man. All this uncertainty, and still he smiles and is friendly and kind. There is no hurry for Marina now – she has time on her hands. The man has no work – the wind is too strong. They sit in agreeable silence watching the waves whip up outside the little harbour. Where they sit is sheltered. They watch a dog wander around the boats pulled up on the shingle. It sniffs at the prow of one boat and is surprised by a cat that is lazing in the sun. The cat leaps up on all fours, fluffs out its tail to a ridiculous size and lashes at the dog, which whimpers and backs off. Marina and the man laugh, and they continue to sit. After a while he points out a starfish to her. A while after that she pats him farewell on the knee as she stands and she wanders back to Zoe's.

Chapter 9

Marina slips the key under Zoe's door. It is too early to wake her.

The taxi boat is waiting in the little harbour as she has arranged. The captain looks sleepy, but his shirt is ironed and today he has polished grey leather shoes with quite pointed toes. To Marina they look modern, but she suspects by the shine of the polish that he has had them for some time.

'Good morning, my lovely lady friend.' He smiles and offers his hand for her to board.

'Good morning, captain. I am glad the wind has died down.'

'Me too. Today I will be busy taking all the stuck people to where they want to be.'

He slides into his leather armchair, starts the engine, and then turns to give Marina a curious smile before he switches on the radio mounted in a plywood box and Greek music fills the cabin. Marina laughs and wags a finger at him to let him know she will still not dance with him. He dances by himself all the way across, one hand on the wheel.

When he pulls alongside the pier at the mainland and throws a rope over the bollard, the music is still playing. He takes Marina's bag on shore and, as she begins to climb off the boat, he spreads his arms horizontally and, with an *'Opa!'*, begins to dance, circling Marina as she reaches for her bag.

'One last dance to remember me by?' he teases Marina.

'For goodness' sake, I am old enough to be your mum, and besides I will be back in a day or two.'

'Lady, you will dance with me at my wedding, for then you will not be able to say no to me and my bride!' He winks at her, jumps aboard, and is off.

Marina watches him go, thinking what a pleasant man he is. She looks across to the island and tries to picture what his fiancée will look like. Far across the water, the hydrofoil pulls out of the harbour.

'Panayia mou! Eleni could be on that.' She scrabbles for her car keys.

She thanks God that the car starts first time, and she heads over the hills for home.

The road is narrow and winding, over the mountains and through olive groves, and it takes a long time. As she approaches the village her stomach begins to rumble. She has had no breakfast. Never mind, it is only another five or six kilometres. She rounds a bend with thoughts of fresh bread, olive oil, and oregano…

A herd of goats blocks the road ahead. Marina slows and tries to edge past but there are too many of them; she will have to wait. She looks around for the goat herder and his dog but they are nowhere to be seen. The goats amble at a lazy pace, stopping to eat

111

from a bush here, standing still for no apparent reason there, and eyeing her blankly. Marina figures that they are being taken either from pasture or to it. Either way, they will turn off the road soon.

But they continue on the road, and Marina glances anxiously at the clock in the car. Time is passing and the goats are showing no signs of concluding their stately meanderings. Marina hoots her horn. The goats at the back turn to look at her and then continue on their way unperturbed. Marina revs the engine and drives as close as she dares to their tails. The ones nearest her skit and jump, but the herd still continues its leisurely pace, stopping for a bite to eat at will.

At this rate Eleni's bus will be in the village before her. She edges even closer to the goats and slowly they begin to part. The car crawls forward into the sea of white, black and tan. The goats nearer the front have long curling horns. Marina decides that her haste is more important than the car's paintwork. She revs and honks and finally breaks free in front of the bleating tide.

She increases the pressure on the accelerator and takes off, but behind the sweet papers and the packets of cable ties on her dashboard there is a red light. She sweeps the wrappers onto the floor and throws the cable ties in the back. The dial indicates that the engine is overheating. Crawling at a snail's pace through the goat herd was too much for the old car. The indicator is on the edge of the red section. Marina changes up a gear, hoping that this will ease the pressure on the engine and the speed will cool everything down, but the needle goes even higher.

She has gone all of two or three hundred metres ahead of the goats when, reluctantly, she is forced to pull over. She releases the bonnet catch and gets out. The day is hot but the greater heat emanating from under the bonnet is immediately apparent. She opens it up and clicks the support bar to hold it. The temperature of the engine is fearsome to Marina's hands, which she waves over it. She has no idea what to do. The radiator cap is too hot to touch. She must only be about four or five kilometres away from the village. Nevertheless, four kilometres will take her over an hour to walk. Maybe there is a more direct route through the orchards.

The sound of goat bells tells her they have caught up and are just behind her around the last corner. The clonking of different-pitched bells accompanying the bleating is normally a sound she likes, but today it is not welcome. A dog is the first to be seen; then comes the herdsman. Marina wonders where they have appeared from. His knees bend out sideways and his trousers are held up with string. His hair is greased back. He leans his weight with each step on the crook he holds. Marina vaguely recognises him from the next village. One of the Malakaopoulous family, perhaps.

He slows his very steady pace as he draws alongside her. He drawls out a lazy long hello. Marina replies automatically, but then asks if there is a way to her village directly through the fields.

113

'You want to go to the village, you say? Well...' He considers at length. 'If I were going to the village, I wouldn't start from here. No, you'd be better off starting away over that hill there.'

Marina is not in the mood for banter. She grabs her bag from the car and strides off along the road. The goats behind her turn onto a narrow lane and the sound of their bells diminishes until all she can hear are the birds in the bushes on either side of the road. She walks faster.

She wonders if Costas will have the sense not to tell Eleni where she has been. Maybe the bus takes longer than she thinks. If it goes to all the little villages on the way maybe she still has time, if she hurries.

There is a clattering sound behind her and a hoot. She turns to see a tractor. Maybe she can catch a lift. She waves for it to stop, but as it draws near she sees it is the goat herder driving. He is grinning mischievously.

He points, with his thumb, to the flatbed trailer his tractor is pulling. Marina smiles, and using the rim of one of the tyres climbs up and sits in the middle with her legs straight out in front of her. There is a strong smell of goat and little pellets of goat droppings are rolling around on the surface of the trailer.

The driver sets the tractor in motion, and as soon as they have gained some speed Marina finds the movement is bouncing her slowly towards the back of the trailer, where she is in danger of falling off.

There is nothing to hold on to but the edge. She grips this with one hand and, with her arm through the handle of her bag, pushes the tips of the fingers of her other hand into a crack in the wooden boards. She is just beginning to feel stable when the herdsman increases the speed and the trailer begins to bounce along the road as it hits pebbles and rocks and potholes.

To Marina's anguish, the bouncing is so violent that it is transferred through her body. She can feel every ounce of her that is not muscle or bone being quivered like a jelly. Worst of all, her support bra's elasticity is giving its contents an animated life of their own. She prises her fingers from the crack in the board and folds her arm across her chest, which gives her immediate relief from the chafing. But she begins a rather rapid traverse towards the back edge and she is forced to give herself up to the movement, no matter how uncomfortable it is, and hold on for dear life.

Marina tries to look ahead to see how far they have to go. The tractor has round reversing mirrors and it is in one of these that she can see the driver looking at her predicament with amusement. Marina tries to turn her back to him, which she eventually manages, and just as she thinks they are making good progress he stops suddenly, splaying her supine.

'I'll be going down this track, then,' he shouts over the tractor engine.

Marina wriggles to the edge of the trailer and slides herself off to the ground. The solidity of the earth is most welcome. The man drives off without even a wave and Marina wishes him good riddance. She straightens her skirt and smooths her blouse. Parts of her feel a bit sore. Nevertheless, she sets off at a brisk pace and within five minutes she is on the main road into the village. When she is just in sight of the square, she hears a low engine noise behind her; as she turns, she can see the bus coming into the village.

Marina breaks into a trot, a very unfamiliar activity. She takes small steps very rapidly and holds her bag in both hands to stop it swinging too wildly. The bus overtakes her and pulls up at the square in front of her, and people begin to get off. Marina darts into the road behind the bus as she sees Eleni climb off and go round to the luggage compartment. By the time Marina passes the bus, the luggage compartment doors have been opened on both sides and Marina can see Eleni's legs on the other side of the bus as she waits for her bag. She recognises Eleni's luggage. On her side of the bus it is the nearest bag to her; on Eleni's side it will be the last to be reached. Marina reaches for the bag and pulls it around the central pillar, hoping to make its extraction from Eleni's side just that bit time-consuming.

She tries running again, and, holding her bag up to hide her face, she darts in front of the bus, across the road that enters the square from the left, and into her shop on the far corner.

'I have not been away. I have been here all the time,' she hisses at a very surprised Costas.

'Go! Go!' she adds, and Costas lazily stands and begins to stretch. 'No time for that, go through the house.' She pushes him in the small of the back, out into the courtyard that connects her house to the shop. As the door swings shut behind him she sits solidly in her chair behind the counter and picks up the order book and a pen. Putting the end of the pen in her mouth she tries to assume the appearance of someone who has been there for hours.

'Mum.'

'Oh – hi, Eleni, is the bus late? I have been waiting ages.'

'How can you have been waiting ages when you didn't know what time to expect me and you sit here all day anyway?' She leans over the counter to kiss her mother on each cheek, an all-but-formal greeting, no warmth. 'And why do you smell of goats?'

Marina realises that, thanks to her hasty dismissal of Costas, she now has to sit in the shop all day and will not get to spend any time with her daughter unless Eleni will sit in the shop with her, something she hasn't done since she was about fifteen. Marina doesn't bother to ask.

Eleni wheels her bag out of the door into the courtyard towards the house, and that is all Marina sees of her for the rest of the day. She closes the shop at midnight and goes through to the house, where Eleni is asleep on the sofa.

Marina stands and stares, takes her in, absorbs all she can. She is so tiny, like a bird, one leg curled under her, the other extended the length of the sofa, one arm bent under her head, the other dangling. Her jeans are slightly too big and her hair is shiny and smooth – she must have just washed it. It falls over her face, flecks of gold in the deep chestnut.

Marina makes her way towards her room but pauses to strokes Eleni's hair softly, her feelings heightened in the action that has been denied her for years. All her rejected love bubbles to the surface. She wants to wrap her arms around her daughter, she wants her to be a baby again so she can scoop her up and take all her fears and anger away for her. Her love seems bottomless. Tears spill over.

'I love you no matter how angry you get,' she whispers, and Eleni sleeps peacefully on.

Eleni has moved sometime in the night. Marina passes her room on her way to the courtyard; the door is open and Eleni is just flopped on top of the bed, fully dressed. At this early hour there is a chill in the air and she is curled into a ball. Marina tiptoes across the wooden boards, takes a blanket from the chest under the window and arranges it over her sleeping princess. She is about to stroke her hair but retracts her hand as the dreamer turns.

In the shop, most of her customers welcome her back but Marina insists she has not been anywhere, just spring-cleaning her home. Some of the women invite her to their houses to do the same, suggesting that they will run the shop in exchange. Marina loves to laugh and has a fun morning. Business grows slack towards midday and Marina has time to think.

All she can focus on is that it is imperative to stop Eleni's relationship, if it is with the person she fears it might be. The pain of being on the island herself when she was young floods back. If only she had the name of the family. She considers the option of telling all she knows, but some words she cannot speak, some pain she cannot face. But could she face it for the sake of her daughter's happiness? Yes, she could. But if she is wrong and Eleni's lover is from another family, which is highly likely, then her words may create the final severing rift and then Eleni will be gone.

No, she is right in what she is doing. She must find out quietly who he is, and only if her fears are borne out will she tell Eleni everything. Then she must tell all, and her own happiness will be secondary, even if it causes a rift that never heals. But if it is not that person, then she can quietly bow out and hope that time will bring her and her beloved daughter back together again. Maybe grandchildren will help? When Eleni understands what it is to be a mother, and Marina can show how much she cares through her love of the grandchildren, maybe then they can reach each other.

'Mum, are you in here all day or is Costas coming in?' Eleni bursts through the courtyard door into the shop. Her hair is fuzzy from sleep and her T-shirt neck is so wide it has fallen down one shoulder. She hitches it back up.

'Costas is coming in about…' Marina turns to look at the clock on the wall, which has a sticker on marking its price, still in drachmas. She has thought of changing it but, with recent events, she thinks she might as well leave it. They may have the drachma again soon enough. 'Well, about now. Why, my love?'

'I dunno, I just thought seeing as I am here we could have a chat or something.' Eleni looks everywhere around the shop but at her mother. She selects a packet of crisps and opens them. Marina opens her mouth to suggest a proper breakfast but then closes it again. She tries out a few replies in her head and judges Eleni's possible reaction to each. Eleni concentrates on her crisps and Marina tries to speed up her thoughts but finds no answers she can feel sure will not cause a negative reaction.

'Morning.' Costas wanders in. Marina stands and Eleni disappears through the courtyard door. Marina turns her mind to the shop's business and runs through with Costas which customers came in this morning short of money and owe them a euro or two. Anything less than a euro she ignores. Nor will she ask for what she is owed; it is up to the discretion of the customer. Every customer is a friend, a neighbour. If a euro is forgotten at the shop it will be paid back with fresh eggs one day, or a lift into town another day. It all evens out in the end.

But she keeps the book in order to appear to take the loan seriously. She has found it makes her customers feel more at ease if she writes it down and crosses it off when, or if, it is paid back. Costas settles into her chair and takes out his phone. As Marina opens the door to the courtyard she can hear the phone whistle and ping as Costas plays a game.

Eleni is in the courtyard sitting under the fig tree, a coffee on the table.

'You want one?'

Marina nods and goes inside herself and pours a coffee. She takes a deep breath before returning to the courtyard.

There is a cat on the wall watching a bird on the roof of the house. The cat picks its way across the jasmine that covers the wall. The jasmine needs watering, but not now. Marina sits in a canvas chair with wooden arms and balances her coffee on her knee to wait for it to cool a little.

'Mum?'

'Yes?'

Eleni's eyes are looking at the ground, darting left and right. Marina can see that she is struggling to form her sentence and wishes she could help.

'What is it, my love?' Marina can think of no other way to help.

'Look, if you had a secret, or knew something that would affect me deeply, make me unhappy even, would you tell me in hopes that we could work it out?'

Oh my God, Panayia, she knows! Oh how in heaven has she found out? Marina can feel her face being drawn white; her hands start shaking and she spills her coffee. The heat penetrates her skirts and, as her knee burns and she jumps in pain, she knocks the tiny cup and saucer onto the floor. To her surprise, Eleni jumps up to help. She picks up the broken pieces, her head so close to Marina's knees she could reach out and touch her silky hair. Marina's hand hovers but she dare not touch. She wants to pull her daughter to her, hug her and protect her, tell her she is sorry.

'I'll get you another.' Eleni is gone.

How could she know? No one knows. Those that did know are dead. Aunt Efi. Even if Eleni's boyfriend is who Marina thinks he could be, he would not tell, he could not tell – could he? No, he would not, could not. No, he is not the source. Besides, if he was, Eleni would be angry, not enquiring. She would be demanding, furious.

Could it be that Eleni has found out about her being on the island, asking questions? That is possible. But she would just think her mother was interfering. She would think it was no more than that – there would be no reason to think there was more to it than that. Short of Marina talking in her sleep and Eleni taking notes, this makes no sense. Does she talk in her sleep? No, it must be that Eleni knows she has been on the island. Panayia! But no, that does not make sense either. Again, she would be angry, not sitting here trying to form sentences. Marina feels slightly light-headed.

'Here you go, Mum.' Marina pulls her chair up to the table so she doesn't have to balance her coffee again. She doesn't trust herself. She has no idea what to say to Eleni but she must say something, think as she speaks, maybe.

'I–' But Eleni does not wait for Marina to say any more.

'Let me put it another way. If I had a secret, or knew something that would affect you deeply, even make you unhappy, would you want me to tell you so we could talk about it – you know, until we felt OK?'

Marina is about to say 'Yes, of course', but then wonders if it is a trick. No, Eleni is not that cunning. Angry, yes – cunning, no. But hang on, if it is not a trick then whom is she talking about? Does she know or not? Perhaps Eleni really has a secret. Marina's brain feels as if it is swelling and the pressure in her head blurs her vision. She takes a sip of coffee, hoping the sweetness will give her clarity. She takes a breath and wills her voice not to give away her panic, her confusion.

'What are you saying, my love?' Marina tries to say the words as gently and kindly as she can, not wishing to scare Eleni away. She needs a little more information to know how to respond. Her voice quivers and sounds breathless. God knows, even talking at this level is such a leap forward for them.

So precious, even if the topic is one she would rather she did not have to discuss.

'Well, if I… if there was… there are… Not everyone…'

What is she trying to say? Eleni's pain is clearly internal. This is about Eleni, not her. If this is about Eleni, why would she come to talk to her now, before she is about to move to the island, unless…? Of course, this must be about the move, maybe about her boyfriend, but not in the way that is connected to Marina. Something else, perhaps. Perhaps they have had a fight? *Oh no, not so soon, poor Eleni.*

'Have you argued with your boyfriend?' Marina tries to help.

'Oh, for goodness' sake, Mum, that's my point exactly, that's why we don't talk! You have only one way of thinking.' Eleni's frustration bubbles over and she stands abruptly. Her thigh jogs the table and both coffee cups tip over in their saucers. But Eleni is in the house, the door slammed behind her. Marina is left to watch the coffee puddle on the table and form rivulets that flow across the table to the stone slab floor.

Marina is ashamed. She is such a coward. She has let Eleni down.

Chapter 10

Marina finishes writing the card. She sighs and puts it with the present, which is already wrapped. She stands wearily, even though it is only mid-morning, and takes the present and card into her bedroom and puts them in her black holdall. She straightens the sheet on her bed. It is the brass bed that belonged to Manolis's mother before her. She would like a modern one with a harder mattress. Although her shop supports her and the girls there is no spare money for such things. She can see herself serving in the shop until the day comes when she cannot get out of bed. With Artemis in Athens and Eleni barely talking to her, the future looks a little bleak.

She hears a door bang. She carefully fastens the clasp on the holdall before leaving the room, shutting the door behind her. She can hear Eleni in the kitchen running a tap. Marina's heavy tread echoes on the wooden stairs. She takes a breath before turning towards the kitchen.

Eleni slams her glass down, and water slops over the top and down her hand. She flicks her wrist at

Marina and the droplets land on Marina's nose and cheeks. Before she can react, Eleni is shouting.

'Why? Why, for God's sake? What for? Just to interfere, to be nosey, what did you think you would find out? You can't even' – she adds an expletive, Marina gasps – 'talk to me, so what's the point in…' Eleni makes a sweeping movement with her hand, generalising and dismissing everything in one gesture.

Marina blinks rapidly and tries to work out what is going on.

'Eleni, my sweet…'

'I am not your sweet, I haven't been for some years, in case you haven't noticed. Just tell me why?'

'Why – what, my love?' Marina wonders if the pain in her chest is the onset of a heart attack. Tears spill down her cheeks and there is a lump in her throat.

'Why did you go to the island?'

Marina swallows hard. 'You weren't meant to know. I was–'

'Yes, I realise that I wasn't meant to know. Costas told me that you weren't telling anyone.'

'Oh Costa, you silly…'

'You call Costas silly? Why? Because he thought your secrets didn't apply to family? So what were you there for, what piece of interference were you planning?'

'Eleni, my precious–'

'You know what, Mum? It doesn't matter. I'm going.'

126

Marina hears her stomp to her bedroom. The general opening and shutting of drawers indicates that she is packing.

Marina knocks quietly. Eleni does not answer. Marina waits. Eleni storms out of her room, past her, bag in hand.

'Eleni, I was trying to save you from some very real pain. If you choose the wrong person–'

'That's for me to decide, it's not up to you who I choose.' Eleni strides past her into the outhouse and pulls her wet washing from the machine.

'No, no. Of course, you must choose, but there is someone there who you must not choose.'

'You see, you have just proved my point! In one sentence you say yes, I must choose, but I must not choose those that you decide are not right. It is just hypocrisy, Mum. You say one thing and mean another. Like you say you want me to be happy, but only under your terms. I can be happy with so-and-so's son, and only if I make the babies that you want. There is only one scenario for you. Any permutation of this and you are interfering. Artemis said that you hardly left her and Sotos alone to get on with their courtship, spying out of windows, arranging for his family to come over for Easter, and dinners. For our sake, just back off.' She takes a breath as she stuffs the wet washing violently into her bag. 'I don't know why I bothered coming home, let alone thinking I could talk to you.' She finishes bundling her washing into her bag. Marina is concerned it will make all her other clothes wet.

'Let me get you a plastic bag for your washing.'

Eleni stands straight, fists bunched, shaking. She stamps her feet and lets out a growl before sweeping up her bag and grabbing her coat from the back of the door. She dumps her things outside the courtyard door and returns, past Marina, into the hall. She closes the partitioning door between them, and Marina can hear the jingle of the phone being picked up.

Artemis has never said a word to her about this. She was just helping, she wasn't interfering. Her lower lip pushes out and she feels it tremble. This is not what she wanted at all. Artemis telling Eleni that she interfered; why did she not talk to her directly?

Marina doesn't wish a bad marriage on either of her children. She knows what a loveless marriage is like. Artemis has already suffered one failed marriage, before she was even twenty-two, and she has the very heavy burden of not being able to have children. It is natural, Marina reasons, for a mother to try to help. She knew Sotos would adore Artemis – he did and does adore her, she was right. But if Artemis has talked to Eleni about her interfering then she has not been right. A tear drips from her chin and she watches it create a dark circle on the stone flags, pushing out a tiny rim of dust.

In the quiet she can hear the tone of Eleni's voice. She has quietened: whomever she is speaking to is soothing her. Marina takes a small step closer to the dividing door. Eleni's voice is muffled. She can make out '*S'agapo*' – 'I love you' – every now and again.

But what she hears most is a quiet, light tone from Eleni that she has not heard for years. She sounds deeply content and just a little playful. Marina takes a deep breath, her throat unconstricts and her chest expands. Her lip stops wobbling and she lightens with a joy that only the well-being of a loved one can bring. She prays to her god that this person is safe for Eleni to love.

The door opens suddenly and Marina steps back.

'Listening in now? Hear anything you want to interfere with?' Eleni brushes past her out into the courtyard, and through the side door. Marina hurries after her. She is standing at the bus stop.

'Eleni, please don't leave. Let's talk about this?'

'Just leave me alone.'

Marina can see Vasso inside the kiosk leaning forward to get a better view.

'Eleni, please?'

'I am going to the island, I don't need to stay here.'

The lady in the pharmacy by the bus stop moves towards the window, her arms folded over her white coat. Stella, the lady who runs the fast-food shop, has turned in her chair outside her shop. She takes a long suck on the straw in her frappé. Marina thinks that she of all people should understand the importance of making a good match. Stella's husband is a pig. Marina turns back to Eleni.

'Come back inside a minute?'

The bus pulls round the corner into the village.

Eleni picks up her bag. Marina feels a wave of panic.

'Eleni, there is something very important I have to tell you. It is imperative for your future happiness.'

'You have about two seconds before the bus stops.'

'I can't tell you here on the street, it is–'

The bus's hydraulics hiss as the baggage compartment opens.

'I will give you a lift. Just come inside now, it is very important. Please Eleni? We need to talk.'

But Eleni throws her bag into the hold and the door closes on it as she mounts the stairs into the bus.

Marina catches the back of her jacket. Eleni pulls it free with a fierce look. 'I tried, Mum! Remember that!' she hisses. The door closes and the bus pulls away.

Vasso sits back in her chair and turns to her television screen. The lady in the pharmacy rearranges things in her window. Stella stands to go inside as a car pulls up in front of her door.

Marina tries to control herself and scuttles back into her courtyard. Costas calls her from the shop but she ignores him. She rushes to her bedroom, picks up her holdall, and, hugging it to her chest, she flings herself on the bed, letting out a loud wail.

'Right, Costa, I am going to see a friend in Athens. I may be gone a while.' Marina has arranged for Mrs Sophia to take on Costas's afternoon shifts, and

Costas is glad of the extra money he will make doing Marina's long shifts.

Costas nods his head but does not look up from his phone. Marina throws her hands up in despair. It is bad enough not making any profit with all this, but it is worse that she has to worry too.

'Costa!'

'What? Yes, you are going to Athens and Kyria Sophia will do my shift. There is to be no credit over five euros, and the man is coming tomorrow to look at the fridge that is on the blink. You will be back when you are back.'

'And make sure you charge the Albanians, Russians, Romanians, Pakistanis, you know, all that lot, an extra ten cents on beer because they never bring the bottles back.'

'Will do... Yes! I am on the next level!' Costas shows the phone screen to Marina, who ignores it.

She goes back to the courtyard and waters the jasmine. She returns to the shop and locks the door to the courtyard and leaves by the shop door. She walks around to the garage where her car waits for her. The mechanic is not there but the keys are in the ignition; she'll pay him when she gets back. She is just driving away when she sees him returning in her rear-view mirror. He waves at her cheerfully and Marina honks her horn – twice, because it's such a good sound. He was very kind to retrieve her car from where she abandoned it and to fix it so quickly.

From Marina's village, halfway to where the taxi boats dock to take people to the island, there is a village large enough to have two clothes shops. The first half of the journey has passed swiftly, but Marina is glad to pull the car to a stop outside one of the shops, the one with clothes in the window that do not look too extreme. What the girls wear these days shocks Marina. She thanks heaven Artemis and Eleni do not dress like that.

Looking in the changing-room mirror Marina cannot believe it is her. For so long she has worn nothing but black. The shift dress in pale blue the lady has offered actually looks very nice, but quite ridiculous with her old black shoes and black socks.

It is also a bit surreal. It is like carnival, dressing up, a disguise.

She buys some blue ankle socks and throws her old black ones in the bin.

Marina feels like a peacock in her finery and struts her way back to the car.

The rest of the journey passes in a variety of daydreams involving her blue dress.

She parks the car and, still with a bit of a swagger, takes her black holdall down to the pier and sits on the bench.

The island is misty blue, undefined, floating like a mirage in the heat. The water is smooth, beckoning with beauty, giving the illusion that she could swim there. Actually she would quite like to swim in the sea. Perhaps there will be time once she is on the island.

The sun shines without a care, lazy, hot. No sound except the lap of the water and, thank goodness, there are no snuffling stray dogs. The island lies in the distance. Not as threatening as the last time. This time it's just a job that must be done. No memory-bubbles of the past bursting to the surface. This time her memories are diluted with the present danger of Eleni recognising her. Eleni's needs eclipse her own, whatever the personal cost. She must do what she must do, and there is just no avoiding it. It is not interfering – it really is a mission of mercy, albeit at the cost of Eleni's being irreconcilably furious with her.

She can see the taxi boat setting out from the island. She watches it as it grows nearer. It is not until it is quite close that she recognises it as the one her friendly dancer drives. She must find out his name. Such a nice young man.

He pulls alongside the pier and Marina stands with a smile. The boat, she notices, is called *Hera*. He does not greet her.

'Won't be leaving for five minutes, lady.'

'Maybe we could dance the time away?'

'Sorry?' He turns to look at her. 'Ah! Is that you? Oh my, would you look at you, all dressed up like a peacock! My, oh my, you take a man's breath away! Come here, pretty lady, and give me a twirl! So fine! And to what honour do we owe this transformation?'

Marina giggles and keeps her head down, feeling quite bashful.

'Oh! Uh oh!'

Marina looks up at the negative sound the man is making. He gives her a sideways glance, and tuts and shakes his head.

'What?' Marina asks.

The man makes an exaggerated head movement to look down at her shoes. She too looks down at the old, worn, black, flat boats on her feet.

'Well, they are comfortable!'

'Lady, you are like a peacock with clogs on! Wait!'

He jumps into his boat and Marina can see seats being lifted, the man scrabbling in the storage areas underneath.

He comes back smiling, swinging something in each hand, and throws one of them at her feet.

It is a leather flip-flop with coloured plastic jewels stuck on the top. Marina laughs and shakes her head.

'Try them.'

Marina peels off a sock and pushes her foot into the flip-flop. The thong between her toes feels very odd but not uncomfortable. She stands and looks down. She cannot deny that, even in all their crudity, they look better than her old shoes.

'Now why would you be travelling with ladies' shoes in your locker?' she asks.

'Why would ladies I keep taking from harbour to beach and back again not be taking them with them, I wonder?'

'You mean they forget them?'

'Bags, shoes, jackets, towels – I could open a shop!'

'No, you wouldn't want to do that.' Marina walks up and down the harbour. The flip-flop is very comfortable.

'I'm afraid they are last year's style, but at least that assures you no one will claim them!' He throws the other one, which lands at her feet. She pushes her other shoe off and peels off her sock and pushes her toes into the gem-encrusted creation.

'They're great!' She wishes she hadn't spent money on the blue socks now.

'Are you going across for the festival?' He offers her his hand to help her on board and lowers her bag in after her.

'What festival?'

'Panayia, mother of God, this is the biggest night of the year. We celebrate the island's most famous captain who single-handedly defeated the Turks in the War of Independence!'

'Single-handedly? Along with the Greek army and navy, and every man, woman and child!'

'Well, he defeated a lot of pirates and sank Turkish ships. Anyway, it's a good show and I will be in it! I will be part of the Greek fleet, attacking the Turkish galleon.'

'What? On the water?'

'Just find yourself a good view of the harbour after it goes dark, then wait and see!' The engine engages and his chair swivels and bobs. He leans across and flicks the switch on his plywood box. The Greek singer Anna Vissi joins them in the boat, the captain singing in his own tongue, loud and proud.

He takes Marina straight to the little harbour so the walk to Zoe's is much shorter. The walk feels familiar and the steps up to the rooms are welcoming. She anticipates a warm reception.

Zoe is very excited to see her, and Roula wants to try her dress on. Uncle Bobby keeps trying to wolf-whistle, but manages little more than a dribble of saliva on his chin. Zoe cuts them all a salad of tomatoes and cucumber and she spoons from a pan of butter beans in a tomato sauce. She pauses her spoon over Marina's plate.

'*Gigandes?*' she asks. Marina nods and Zoe spoons.

'I had an uncle once who had a restaurant in Athens,' Marina begins as she tears a slice of bread off the half-cut loaf. 'One day he was serving *gigandes* and someone called out that there was a cockroach in his bowl of beans. My uncle realised that if it was a cockroach he was finished. Everyone in the taverna had heard the complainer and it would only be a matter of time before word spread across Athens. The customers turned to see what my uncle would do.' Marina forks a bean and it hovers by her mouth. 'So he walked over to the customer who had complained, and looked into his dish. He saw the black thing in the beans and with his fingers he quickly picked it out and ate it. "It's just a burnt bean!" he declared, and no one could argue because the evidence had gone.' Marina pops the bean into her mouth as if to re-enact the story. Roula laughs through her nose and puts her paper serviette over her mouth. Zoe, who has put down the pan of beans, slaps her aproned thighs and laughs, throwing her head back. Bobby nearly chokes.

The lunch lasts until mid-afternoon and finally everyone is feeling sleepy. Bobby is already asleep. The aunt still hasn't woken up and Marina wonders how she can be so big if she is never awake to eat. She helps clear the plates before picking up her bag and taking her leave.

It feels good to be back in the rented room. 'My room!' Marina chortles to herself. 'It is amazing how quickly we become familiar.' This leads to a series of thoughts about Eleni becoming too familiar with the wrong person. She pulls the list out of her bag.

Costas Voulgaris – The Cockerel – because he was noisy – Father owned kafeneio by the port.

Panayotis (Panos) – His father was a barber. Yiayia has seen young Panos walking past the house.

Socrates Rappas – Always fiddling with things, quiet.

Yannis Harimis – Known as 'Black Yanni' because he is so brown in the summer – his Yiayia was the midwife.

Aris Kranidiotis – Very naughty – his sister married the papas from the church across on the mainland.

Apostolis (Tolis) Kaloyannis – His father owned the boatyard on the mountain village path.

Alexandros Mavromatis – She says he made her laugh. Known as 'The Butterfly' for his flitting from one girl to the next.

She has drawn a line through Panos and Yannis.

The *kafeneio* owner's son should be easy to find, and the boatyard man's son.

Also, Panos was such a sweetie and she really did enjoy her brief visit to him, so she thinks she might return to him and ask him if he knows the other people on her list. She suspects he is good at discretion. Maybe he could also cut her hair? And she liked the girl: cool, calming. Interesting people.

After her afternoon sleep Marina takes the back route across to the main town and down to the harbour. She passes what she now thinks of as Aunt Efi's place, without too much heartache. She passes the little shop that has spread onto the narrow lane. Further along there is a crossroad of paths with a shop almost as cluttered as her own, but with no goat bells or shepherd's crooks, although it does have exotic fare such as brown bread and avocados.

It is all downhill after that. Shallow steps and steep steps, winding and turning. Dodging onto the shady side as she turns corners. Some of the houses near the port are now used as shops. Nothing has really been done to effect this conversion. The windows remain house windows, but the front doors stand open. Electrical goods crowded into a space as big as her own front room. Galleries, all clinical and white with odd, nonsense paintings, splodges and drips, that sort of thing. A bookshop which looks as if it never opens, with a mobile phone number pinned to the door.

Round the corner and the final lane. Tourist goods on narrow benches in front of shops create an aisle that leads to the heightened sights and sounds and smells of the port itself.

Ropes slap rhythmically against the masts of the yachts; the port is no less busy than when she left. Now there are some larger boats anchored on the outside of the far pier, too large to enter the crowded harbour. The goods boat is in, its wide rear metal gangway laid flat onto the stone quay and its guts emptied of cargo. A few cats sit contentedly licking their paws. Maybe there were some fish on board.

'How do?' A gruff voice addresses her. Marina turns to see Yanni disappearing up the lane she has just come down. He has sacks of sand, or possibly cement, roped onto his beast.

'Hi!' Marina calls, but he has gone and her voice blends with the harbour noises.

'Hello there!' Another cheerful welcome. Marina turns again to see the other donkey man she met, smiling away as he walks towards her, his mules laden with six-packs of drinking-water bottles, his hair carefully combed over.

'*Kalimera!*' Marina smiles in return before he passes.

Marina feels almost as if this is a home from home. For a moment she enjoys the familiarity, until she catches sight of herself in a shop that has a mirror for trying on sun hats outside. The blue dress shocks her. Suddenly she feels conspicuous. What's more, the donkey men have recognised her. She scuttles into the nearest shop to ensure Eleni doesn't have a chance to see her if she is around.

A woman offers her assistance. Marina looks at the hats as her excuse for being there. She finds a dark-blue, very wide-brimmed hat. She tries it on and it flops over her face. The assistant offers her something with a neater brim but Marina is pleased with the effect. She decides that even she would not recognise herself in her new dress with this hat on. She says she will take it and the woman takes out a calculator to work out the price.

'Do I look like a tourist?' Marina is dumbfounded at the cost. The woman blushes. Marina tells her she has her own shop and she understands about markup but there has to be a line drawn somewhere for Greek people who are just trying to get by. The woman blushes a second time and stabs more buttons on her calculator. She comes out with a price that, to Marina, is still high but much more reasonable. She hands over the money and the woman takes the note but not the coins. Marina smiles. The woman smiles back, looking more comfortable now.

Marina puts the hat on as she leaves the shop and pulls the brim over her face. She looks along the row of cafés. There is no way of knowing which one Costas Voulgaris's father might own. She wonders whether she should sit at one and then enquire of the waiter, or if she should go into one of the cafés and enquire directly. Coffee is not cheap at the port-side places.

'Hello, *bougatza* and coffee?' a voice asks. It is the waiter from the last time she was here. Marina is amazed how he can possibly remember her from all the people he must serve every day. She also feels a little disconcerted at how easily he has recognised her despite her change of dress and hat. Then she notices her brim has blown back in the breeze, framing her face. Besides, she reasons, Eleni has never seen her in anything but black so she will not take any notice of a middle-aged lady in pale blue. She will just appear to be another person in the crowds. Nevertheless, Marina pulls down the broad brim of the hat. It flops over her face and she feels uncomfortably dramatic.

'Oh, hello. Actually, I am looking for a Costas Voulgaris. Do you know him? His family owns a café down here somewhere.' It is out without a thought.

'Costas Voulgaris, let me think. Ah, Costas! Tell you what, you take a seat and I will bring *bougatza* and frappé. Sweet, wasn't it?' Marina nods. 'And I will tell you all about that rogue Costas Voulgaris!'

Marina cannot help but smile. She selects a chair near to the café so she can see all the chairs in front of her, stretching down to the water's edge. There are one or two tourists but it is mostly empty. There is life everywhere but it is not sitting still. Everyone is moving, carrying, pulling, lifting, serving, talking. Only the cats and the tourists sit.

A hydrofoil pulls into the harbour and generates a bustle of activity down that side of the port. A number of men in suits get off. They look hot but they keep their jackets on.

'Lawyers.' The waiter puts her frappé and *bougatza* in front of her. She looks up at him and he nods to the seat opposite her. She nods in return. He sits.

'How do you know they are lawyers?'

'Who else would wear a suit in this heat? Besides, I happen to know that they are exchanging contracts on a three-million-euro mansion up on the hill there tomorrow, so they have come today to watch the festival tonight.'

'Three million! Why so much?'

'Because all the foreigners want to live here, it drives the prices up. It's an American who is buying the mansion tomorrow.'

'How do you know so much?'

'It is my mansion.'

Marina flinches and tries to reconcile a man with a three-million-euro mansion working as a waiter.

'So is this your last day of work?'

'Now, why would it be my last day of work? What else would I be doing with my day? I sold a taverna last month for over a million.'

'How come you have so much property, and why are you selling it?' Marina has heard such direct questions in Greece all her life, and it seems only natural to ask.

142

'I am from a big family that has grown small. It has all come to me and I am selling it because these crazy prices will not last – how can they? It is not reality, it is madness. So I make my fortune while I can and get rid of things that would otherwise need my attention. Excuse me.' The waiter jumps up and persuades a German couple that they need beer and sandwiches. They sit down by the harbour's edge and the waiter ambles to the café and returns with their drinks, before sliding in opposite Marina again.

'Yes, I am the last in the line and unmarried. After me there are no more Voulgarises when I am gone.'

'Voulgaris as in Costas, by any chance?'

'The rogue himself!' The corners of his mouth twitch with a suppressed smile.

The lawyers make it as far as the café, puffing and sweating in the hot sun, looking incongruous in their suits and sunglasses. They sit at a table near to Marina and talk into their mobile phones.

One of them clicks his fingers for a waiter. 'Excuse me,' mouths Costas, and serves the lawyers, who are demanding and pompous. Marina smiles to herself, picturing their confusion tomorrow in the notary's office when they recognise that the waiter who is serving them now is in fact their client…

She chuckles too at the roundabout way Costas has introduced himself. She allows herself to giggle and then giggles a little longer at the easy way her next question has been set up.

'So, you are the very last? No girlfriends on the horizon?' For a brief second Marina is hopeful. A millionaire son-in-law would take care of her old age.

'There was one, an American girl, but she took herself back to America. What can I do? Such is life.'

'You could go and find her?' Marina swallows her brief disappointment.

'She left because she didn't like it here. She will not return.'

'No, I mean you could live in America.'

'*Panayia mou!* Why would I do that and leave this piece of heaven?' He nods at a donkey dropping its breakfast from under its tail. Then he is up again slickly, sidling up to an English couple. He persuades them to sit for a pot of tea and pancakes. He offers them any chair they like and they settle in next to the Germans by the water's edge. Costas Voulgaris the millionaire goes inside and returns with sandwiches for the Germans, who order more beer. With no sense of hurry he wanders indoors and reappears with a tray of tea things and two beer bottles gripped between his white knuckles. He only bothers to use one hand for the lot, the other swinging freely and limply by his side.

Marina is trying to think what she will say when Costas asks why she wants to know who he is, and fails to come up with anything that sounds both reasonable and discreet. As he passes her table he drops off her bill and a gives her a lazy smile.

He serves the English their pancakes and then disappears for a while. Marina waits. After half an hour she decides to wait no longer. She stands to announce she wishes to pay the bill and a young waiter approaches her.

'Oh, where's Costas?'

'He's playing backgammon inside. Did you need him?'

'Oh, no, it's fine.' She collects her change and wonders whether to leave a tip for the multi-millionaire. She decides not, and begins to leave, but feels mean and turns and slips fifty cents under her plate, after using the table as a rest to cross his name from her list.

Chapter 11

Evening is drawing in. A stage is being set up on the harbour front where the commercial boats come and go. From there, all along the waterfront, including the steps that lead up to the cannons, access to the port has been cordoned off.

Marina wonders if she can find... She stops to consult her list.

Aris Kranidiotis – Very naughty – his sister married the papas from the church across on the mainland.

It's a small island and finding people doesn't seem to be difficult. Marina decides to ask Panos if he knows the four remaining men on the list. She walks towards the corner to turn up the narrow lane that leads to the corridor street where his stairs begin.

The lacemakers are all closing their shops. There is an air of excitement which Marina presumes is for the celebrations. The little old ladies in black carefully fold the lace that has been on display outside and lay the pieces in flat boxes. Marina is interested in looking at some of the lace. The last time she didn't really taken any notice but the piece she ended up buying is very pretty and she has laid it as a centrepiece on her kitchen table.

Marina picks up a piece the lady has not yet folded and holds it up. The lacework around the edges is very fine, the central piece of linen as smooth a satin. Marina lays it back down and is just about to pick up another piece when a movement up the lane catches her attention. Three people are coming out of the very narrow passage where Panos has his barbershop, and Marina immediately recognises her daughter's voice. She doesn't wait to see her face. She pulls the brim of her hat down low and, turning her back, tries to disguise her walk as she scuttles around the corner back onto the port side.

Once there, she does her best to run a few steps before stopping at a sunglasses shop, and in pretence of looking at glasses, sidles around the rack so she can watch the end of the lane she has just come from. She doesn't believe the Ray-Bans are genuine, not at these prices.

Eleni comes around the corner with two girls. Marina realises the relief she would have felt had she come around the corner arm in arm with her young man; then Marina could have found out who he was and laid this whole thing to rest – one way or another. No more deception and silly disguises.

A man approaches her to see if she intends to buy. Marina thanks him kindly and winds her way through the stands of hats, T-shirts and suncream as fast as she can, away from Eleni. She reaches the turn of the harbour that takes her down to the seafront walk around to the smaller harbour. She window-shops from one glass front to another. There are a good many shops selling gold jewellery. Well, if they are all as rich as Costas Voulgaris and his American buyers, then no wonder.

Marina looks at the reflection in the window. She has seen that done in a detective film once. She can see Eleni, who is still coming towards her. She is laughing and seems so relaxed. Marina watches longer than is safe, and darts into the shop as Eleni walks past. She watches through the window. It is so nice to see her daughter happy. Although her trousers are a little shapeless – that's what happens if you bundle them wet into a bag. They need a good iron.

Marina leaves the shop as Eleni progresses along the harbour and is no longer visible through the window. Eleni's movements are so carefree. Marina finds she is following without having made the decision. The girls turn into a *souvlaki* fast-food shop. Marina turns to look in another window. More gold jewellery.

There is a sign in ornate gold writing on a black shiny surface sitting centrally on the velvet window display: *Kranidiotis – Jewellers since 1999*. Marina has to think what year it is, as it seems that the millennium was only yesterday, but she calculates it is twelve years since then. Still, twelve years does not seem a lot to brag about. She wonders how quickly shops come and go along the port.

She hears Eleni laugh. The girls have come out of the fast-food place, each holding a pitta bread wrap containing meat, tomatoes, onions and *tzatziki* – a yoghurt, cucumber and garlic sauce. Marina can see the *tzatziki* dripping over her daughter's fingers; she pauses to hope it doesn't drip onto her clothes, before entering the jeweller's.

'Aristotelis Kranidiotis at your service, madam. How can I help you?'

'Oh, er, hello.' Marina wonders why she recognises his name, but watches Eleni as she passes the window. She is licking the *tzatziki* off her hand whilst trying not to spill any more from her wrap.

'Was it something for yourself or a loved one?'

Marina loses sight of Eleni after she has gone past the window. She turns to the man addressing her. He has an orange glow to his tan and a thick neck. He is wearing a wide orange tie which mirrors his complexion. Marina begins a giggle but puts her hand to her mouth and coughs.

'I'm sorry, what did you say?'

'Aris Kranidiotis at your service. Are you looking for yourself or for a loved one?'

Aris Kranidiotis! But Marina is not all that surprised; Greece has a way of making the right people turn up at the right time. Like the Americans the day she first arrived.

'Now, if it was for a loved one,' she says, 'a daughter, say, twenty-eight years old – or in your case your lover of twenty-eight years old – what would you buy her?'

He laughs heartily. 'First I would have to pay my medical bills for the injuries I would receive, and then for the divorce, if I were to deceive my wife in such a way. But to choose something for my daughter would be easy, although she is eight, not twenty-eight, but girls are girls. They are born with expensive tastes.' He sighs and takes out an oversized handkerchief from his top pocket and wipes his brow, and rubs between his fingers.

Marina notices the yellow ends of his fingers as he replaces the cloth and scrabbles in his shirt pocket for a cigarette, the spreading damp patches under his arms showing all the more clearly for this exertion.

'Actually, I think it's best if I come in with her.'

The jeweller is still trying to get his lighter to work as she closes the door behind her. He succeeds as she turns towards the coast walk, and he waves farewell through the window, smiling and exhaling smoke though his nose.

Marina stops at the fast-food place and takes out her piece of paper. She makes use of one of the small, high circular tables outside and puts a line through Aris's name. Three to go. The easiest one to track will be *Apostolis (Tolis) Kaloyannis – His father owned the boatyard on the mountain village path.* She will get up very early the next morning and walk along to the boatyard.

Tonight she will watch the festival, but first she will return to her room and take a shower. She hopes she does not have sweat showing under her arms. She is glad she doesn't smoke.

Zoe says she has seen the festival many times and is not really keen to go out. Roula says the bangs frighten her, and besides, *Three, Two, One* is on in a minute.

Bobby says he would love to go and would she mind giving him a piggyback. Zoe tells him not to be so cheeky, and Bobby mouths behind her back, 'How's it going?' Marina nods an affirmative. Their attention is drawn as the large aunt, who as far as Marina has observed never moves, suddenly stands, and before Marina can see her face out of repose she turns and slowly waddles off to an inner room, her weight rolling her like a ship in a storm.

'Night, Auntie,' Roula calls. Zoe leaves the room. Apparently putting the aunt to bed is a two-person job.

Marina wishes them a good night, but Bobby has dropped off and Roula is singing the theme tune to her favourite show.

Marina is not sure where to go for a good view of the harbour. She presumes she should be down at the port. She climbs the steep steps to get to the amphitheatre at the top of the main town, from where she can descend to the port. She has come to the conclusion that this way is slightly shorter than going along the coast, and it is certainly better lit by night. As she passes the corner shop at the intersection of paths, she converges with a small group of people who are discussing the best vantage point for the evening's spectacle. They agree that being in the port has its advantages, but higher up gives a panoramic view of the proceedings. They decide on the hill that separates the main harbour from the small harbour. Marina tags on behind, allowing them to lead.

The houses are left behind. The paths they take get narrower, rockier, with low-level spiky plants lining them on either side. The way is no longer lit by lamps on the sides of buildings or attached to whitewashed walls. Illumination comes only from the moon. Two of the party have brought torches and one shines forward, one backward. They climb to near the top of the hill and find a flat area. They each find a rock to sit on or lean against. Marina now feels she is imposing on the group and so, using the light of the moon and caution, continues past them to a small plateau on the very top of the hill. Here, there are one or two others who have also made the ascent. She finds a flat rock and sits. The hill drops away sharply and she can see the port laid out below her like a map. There are, around the stage she saw being erected earlier, bright lights. The rest of the harbour by comparison is in the dark, with only the moonlight on the water distinguishing land from sea.

She waits. Being so high up, she can see both ways along the channel of water between the island and the mainland. Behind her is her favourite view to the open sea. The dotted islands are dark tears in the Prussian-blue sky sitting on the vacillating sea, the shine of the moon on the dark of the sea's own depth flitting across its surface in random interlocking feathers.

On the hilltop a couple are holding hands; another intertwined couple are further away still. It is too dark to make out features. The moon is behind them and they are all shadows. The couple nearest move as if they are young. The other couple are joined as one, only the silhouette of two heads giving the lovers away.

An unexpected screech of microphone feedback draws Marina's attention back to the port. The speakers squeal painfully. She hears one of the couple nearest her on the hill curse God, and his hands go up to his head, presumably over his ears. It is too dark to tell.

The feedback stops and someone taps the microphone. He introduces himself as the mayor and begins what Marina believes will be a very long speech, about the resilience of the people of the island. His words are distorted by an overstrained system as well as the echoes off the rocks and houses.

He is mercifully brief, and Marina crosses herself in thanks. Another voice comes over the speakers. This one is more muffled than the last but speaks in a dramatic tone. Two spotlights come on and scan independently across the town and away up onto the hill. Marina shields her eyes when in full glare, turning her head sideways. The couple next to her are briefly illuminated. It is Panos and his boyfriend. Marina feels happy for them, the cover of the night allowing them some normality in their display of affection towards one another.

The spotlight turns towards the cannon at the top of the steps guarding the entrance to the harbour, and Marina can see men with flaming torches begin a walk down to the quayside where there is a boat with flags and a canopy. The men climb in and the narrator is superseded by a triumphant piece of music by the composer Vangelis, which Marina loves. She recently heard this particular piece in a film on the television in her shop. She tries to think of the film's name but her mind is a blank.

The little boat full of the men is rowed slowly out of the harbour.

'*Chariots of Fire!*' Marina announces, and slaps a hand over her mouth at the unbeckoned sounds.

The little boat is passing the end of the harbour wall, and at this point Marina notices the red and green navigation lights of a dozen small boats out in the open waters. More are joining them as she watches, and Marina guesses every fishing boat and taxi boat on the island must be out there, waiting, in a semi-circle. Marina straightens her back and searches them to see if she can distinguish which one is her friend, the dancing captain. But the sea is dark, and only the lights can be seen.

The spots, which have been tracking the little boat, split, one remaining on the boatload of torch-bearing Greek sailors, and the other scanning across the water until it falls upon what looks for all the world to Marina like an old-fashioned galleon out of a black-and-white film, of the kind with pirates swinging from the rigging.

The music swells and fills the hollow of the town, rippling off the hills, filling Marina's heart. She feels excited and wishes she had a friend with whom to share this experience. She suddenly feels lonely. She wonders if the taxi boat man is single. She contemplates that as you grow older a decade or so's difference in age means less than when you are young. A fifteen-year-old with a twenty-five-year-old is obscene. A seventy-year-old with an eighty-year-old, for example, is sweet. At which end of the continuum would they be?

As the little manned vessel rows closer to the old-fashioned boat, Marina realises that it is not a full-sized ship but a replica with a rowing-boat base. It is flying the Turkish flag, the enemy in the battle being depicted. The rowing boat shines a light to signal to the shore and the music changes to something military. The sound of cannon fire fills the watery arena, and the assembled fishing boats and water taxis put out their red and green lights and with bright flashing lights depict cannon fire aimed at the Turkish vessel. Some let off red flares as they pretend to be fired upon. Marina, loneliness forgotten, is finding it hard to sit still, the music stirring, the sights all-encompassing, the whole of the harbour below her the stage and the townspeople the players. She feels like a goddess. Hera, perhaps, like the name of the dancing captain's boat. Goddess of…? Marina can't quite remember. She scans her school memories. Marriage! Oh well, sort of appropriate. She could not be called interfering if she were a goddess. Marina, goddess of marriage. She chuckles.

Then quite suddenly, amidst the flashing lights, red flares and music, the Turkish boat is on fire. There are no lights creating this; it is no illusion – the boat is ablaze. Marina gasps out loud. She senses that Panos, or his friend, turns and looks towards her but it is too dark for Marina to tell who it is, or for him to see her. She puts her hand over her mouth to gain some control but it slips to her lap as the ship continues to burn, lighting up the fishing boats and water taxis that are now circling like vultures.

Blink. Crack. Marina's hand goes to her mouth. Fireworks explode from the ship. Starbursts and red flares. Rockets and fizzings. Marina's eyes water and she wipes away a tear of fun and fear. As each explosion rips through the ship, the scene below is lit up bright as day, like lightning striking. The music swells. The fishing boats circle menacingly. The ship is sinking now, but still the silver fireworks ignite, the surrounding Greek fleet slowly backing away into the darkness, lights extinguished. The Turkish ship capsizes, the mast dipping into the water, the Turkish flag now beneath the waves, the flames flickering and struggling for life as the water takes their oxygen, until all is dark and still. Marina wants to cheer. But as soon as the feeling comes upon her a series of rocket fireworks are launched from along the harbour's edge. Her emotions are left suspended as a new spectacle unfolds.

156

And then, the rockets gone, silence and dark remain. Not a light, not a sound. The island could be empty.

Out of the silence come the first few bars of a *sirtaki*, Zorba's dance. Steady and slow at the beginning, baram de de de, baram de de de, dropping a tone, baram de de de, baram de de de, and then picking up at a gallop. Marina can no longer help herself and she claps in rhythm, only to find, very quickly, her hands suspended as she is overwhelmed by the firework display of rockets from the harbour exploding in time to the music's beat. As the music gets faster, so do the explosions of silver until the music is played out by coloured fireworks ignited from behind the cannon at the top of the step with nothing but sky for a backdrop. The fireworks are thunderous, bursting overhead in reds and greens and purples, showering the island.

The sky grows wider and wider as the pyrotechnics reach greater heights and explode in a sunflower of colour, only to detonate again in fizzing puffs of spiralling embers. Silver to blue to red, the intensity of light illuminating a lacework of smoke trails drifting in the sky.

One after another, the florets and dandelion clocks of illuminated spectrum fill the sky until the music can no longer be heard for the whizzes and bangs, cracks and whistles. The dome of sky above Marina's head is filled to capacity, each phenomenon being surpassed by the next extravaganza, until the sky is bright with colour and Marina's face shines in the

157

glow, her blue dress reflecting each colour in turn, itself becoming part of the painting. Marina looks down at her hands. They too are changing colour.

Just as she thinks there can be no more, the final earth-shattering bang sends a rocket so high Marina thinks it has extinguished itself, but when it appears to be directly overhead there is an explosion of light followed by the accompanying delayed crack. Each separate spark of this first disgorging flare detonates again, and the night sky is filled with silver rain that falls and falls, trails of white smoke streaking the sky in the aftermath.

One of the boats in the harbour sounds a rude horn in a token of appreciation. This is followed by another and another, the large boats moored outside the harbour wall, blaring their baritones for minutes at a time, smaller vessels parping repeatedly, everyone trying to outdo their neighbour. All around the town, people are whistling.

Marina, hidden in the dark, whistles and whistles, first to show her appreciation but then because she is trying to out-whistle someone on a hill the same height as hers across the harbour. Back and forth they shrill it out, Marina feeling every bit like the naughty child she is enjoying being.

A tap on the microphone is dimly audible in the massive noise the people of the island are making. It brings some order, and the wave of quiet grows until the man on the microphone can be heard thanking this person and that for their contributions to the evening, ending with thanks for the anonymous donation that paid for the fireworks. He names every child who has danced and even sends good wishes to those who could not for whatever reason, mentioning each by name. No one is forgotten, judging by the long list he reads out.

Panos and his friend turn and begin the delicate and careful trek down from the very top as the list of names continues. As they near Marina, Panos acknowledges her and Marina greets them both with a smile and wishes them '*Kalinixta*' – goodnight – although she is aware that for them the night will likely not be over, as they will probably go down to a bar or a friend's house. They pass by, discreetly holding each other's sleeves. The second couple come towards Marina.

Marina quickly bends to the ground and fumbles around in her bag on the floor. She has heard Eleni's voice. This is Eleni and her boyfriend. The desire to look and see who he is tugs at her but she dares not look up. She continues rummaging in her bag and they pass behind her in the dark.

Eleni says, 'Goodnight.'

Such good manners. Marina opens her mouth to reply but takes a second to lower her voice and hold her nose in the dark. The result is she sounds unbelievable, and as if she smokes forty cigarettes a day.

Eleni's friend replies in a light, youthful voice. He doesn't sound thirty-five, which feels like a relief for some reason. After they have passed by, Marina feels safe enough in the dark on the top of the hill to look after them. He is about the same height as Eleni, slim built – lithe, perhaps – and he is offering his hand to help Eleni on every step. Marina instantly likes him for this action alone. Eleni trips and she is caught, and gifted with a kiss. Such tenderness.

Marina tries to hurry down the steep unlit slope to get a better look at him, see his face, but it is treacherous and the hill drops away down to the town on one side. A false step could be fatal. She looks up to see them again. He is wearing a strange hat, but then in the dark everything can seem strange. She focuses on placing her feet until the ground becomes more solid.

She can still see them away in the distance as they turn into the whitewashed passages. Eleni looks so light on her feet, so carefree. They are so similar she could confuse the two at this distance.

Marina makes a mental note that she can now eliminate any of the three men left on her list by height and build. If she had known his dimensions she could have easily ruled out chubby Aris Kranidiotis without even talking to him, as well as the tall millionaire Costas Voulgaris, although she enjoyed his performance. Panos would have almost fitted the bill, although he is perhaps a little tall and with broader shoulders. Eleni's man was narrow top to bottom: a wiry stick, although it feels unfair to judge in the dark, the dark being so deceiving that Eleni didn't even recognise her own stooping, nose-pinching mother.

As soon as she is off the hilltop, the way down to the lit paths seems very quick. Once amongst the houses, Marina makes it back to Zoe's within ten minutes. The house is dark; no sound of the television reaches her as she passes the front door.

Just before Marina turns out the light in her own room she takes her list from her bag and puts a line under Apostolis Kaloyannis. It is late, but if she can get up in time she will walk out to the boatyard before the sun is up tomorrow.

Chapter 12

It is still cool when Marina's little alarm clock rouses her at 5 a.m. For a moment she thinks she is at home and must get up to open the shop. She turns onto her side and pushes herself up, swinging her legs to the floor, which her feet find before she expects it. She sits up straight and leans her weight forward to stand. Only when she is upright does she open her eyes.

The sight of the rented room dispels all thoughts of her shop and she feels tempted to sit back down again, lean over, allow gravity to pull her down to the mattress and curl up to go back to sleep. She even begins to bend her knees to sit, her bottom poised over the mattress edge. But a vision of Eleni from last night focuses her commitment.

Her flip-flops feel cooler than her shoes and most of the creases have dropped out of her dress overnight. She steals into the unbroken dawn with her hat pulled firmly down on her head, but at the last minute she changes her mind about the flip-flops and returns to put on socks and her comfortable old shoes. Much more practical for walking.

The houses are silent, windows wide open to let in the cool night air, black interiors for the sleepers within. Marina is not sure she remembers how to get to the upper road that joins the coastal path heading to the boatyard. She knows she must go behind Zoe's, up the side of the hill, and she trusts she will join the top path that will lead her all the way to the village of five houses with the beautiful beachfront further along the coast road to the western end of the island.

The narrow paths are deceptive in the half-light. They look like public rights of way between houses, but twice Marina finds herself turning a corner into someone's backyard and retracing her steps. It is taking longer than she anticipated just to find the main path she needs. At this rate the dawn will break and the sun will chase into the sky, leaving her return journey heatstroke hot and shadeless. She walks faster until she finally finds the path and sets out at a good pace.

She took this path once before, way back then – Aunt Efi was asleep again and Marina tiptoed down the steps, lifting the door open so the bottom wouldn't scrape, and headed out in the hot afternoon. She found the top way that leads to the coastal path by chance, and when it opened out into a pretty little valley down to the sea Marina felt she was in a different world. Goats grazed in the fields above the path, and donkeys and goats in the field to the right. To Marina's knowledge it is the only working farm on the island; these are the only fields of green. The farmhouse is planted under a rocky outcrop whose top must have incredible views of the sea. However, the farmer must have decided shade was more important and his house nestles into the rock so that its back provides the fourth wall.

Nothing has changed. The smell of goats and the sounds of goat bells tell Marina they are there, but the goats above the path in amongst the scrub and the rocky outcrops blend to invisibility.

The gently undulating field to her right also hosts the sound of goat bells, but they too are invisible. In the middle of the field is a twisted old olive tree, beneath which a white ghost of a horse is tethered, the pre-dawn light melting its outline into the haze. Its head nods as it plucks grass, and its flicking calls to mind the flies that will grow more persistent as the heat increases. Marina presses on, aware that the cool she is enjoying has a limited window.

She can hear a distant voice up on the hill. The silhouette of a man leading four donkeys heads towards the town. Marina wonders why, if he is talking to himself, he is being so loud. He stops. and the donkeys, following his lead, dip their heads to the ground. The man's silhouette turns and Marina can see his arm is raised, he is on his mobile. He sees Marina and waves, and continues to shout down the phone as he turns and resumes his morning trek.

Marina's path begins to drop and the hills slide away to the sea, which has just started to take on a pale silver-orange sheen on its oil-like surface as the sun peeps its first tentative rays over the horizon.

Marina joins the coastal path that is slashed into the hillside, which continues its descent without relenting its curve towards the sea. There are a few houses dotted at this joining of the paths. A small church embraces the hillside, the stone above the door inscribed *1820*.

Past the houses she can see the coastal path stretching along the length of the island. Dawn is breaking over the sea behind her and the path is golden. A black butterfly lands in front of her. It pauses motionless, wings closed, until it darts up to join a friend, circling in dance. The charms of these butterflies have not diminished over the years. She was so taken with them when she was first here that she spent hours while she was stuck in Aunt Efi's apartment embroidering them onto hankies and other things. Always two of them, joyfully circling in depressing black thread. Joyful and depressing, reflecting her ambivalent mood.

Marina, on the level path, increases her speed, her flat black shoes at one with her feet. She watches her feet for a few steps. A small piece of cotton thread sticking up on the toe of her right shoe is new. It looks strangely clean against her old shoes.

The view down the channel is uninterrupted here. There is a small island close to the shore, black against the orange water, with a tiny whitewashed church on top like a piece of royal icing. The island further out is larger, also boasting a church. The island beyond casts a long shadow across the water behind it. Far across the water, a tiny black speck accompanies the low chug of a fishing-boat engine, heading home for breakfast.

Marina makes a note of the sun's advance and looks ahead along the path. She is making good progress but is concerned that she cannot see the path some way ahead at all. She wonders if there has been a landslide. There will be some sort of path, presumably, but the way will become harder.

What Marina thought was a small inlet before the path disappears turns out to be a sizable recess, the path becoming a concrete road as it cuts across the beach to section off the dry bay, sharply scooped out from the steep hills. She has reached the boatyard, and the sun is barely off the horizon. Marina congratulates herself on her speed. Half a dozen little wooden fishing boats have been dragged up onto the shingle beach. On the other side of the wide raised concrete path, inside the yard itself, a few larger vessels are lined up, standing on their keels and propped up by wooden poles on either side, with makeshift wooden ladders dotted liberally where needed. A grand wooden caique, next to a small wooden tug, next to modern fibreglass yacht. The supporting poles look like giant insect legs, a frozen army ready to march, tarpaulins, slung like greatcoats over shoulders, protecting them from the sun as the hulls are caulked and painted. Underbellies half stripped of paint, the underlying wood scorched by the flame-torches of the workmen. A silent platoon of suspended effort. All is still.

To the left of the yard is an impressively large old stone house set into the hill, the covered veranda with its stone arch overlooking the place of work. But all is quiet here too. The shutters closed, abandoned chairs on the patio.

A cockerel crows as if to prove someone lives in the valley's bowl. Amongst the orange and olive trees Marina can see half a dozen low-lying stone houses, blue in this light, their orange roofs burnt dark in the sun, belying their age.

Marina is not sure what to do. A sense of panic grips her chest. The boatyard is clearly packed up for the season. Dry dock is not the place for boats in summer, and it is a wonder there are any here at all.

At the other side of the beach, near the ramp used for hauling the boats in and out of the water, there is a painted notice.

Marina, at a loss for what to do next, and feeling as if her task has become insurmountable, allows her legs to continue their pace until she is standing in front of the notice. It is written on a piece of weathered hardboard with a scratchy marker pen that all but runs out of ink near the end, the letters fading.

Boat Owners, Sailors, Captains and Crew

We love you in the winter when your work is our business…

We love you in the summer when by chance we meet and share sailing stories over an ouzo…

167

But if you have a work-related problem in the heat of the summer, ask yourself if it can wait till we reopen in the less hot months before you call us or walk up to our house in the mountains where you will find us enjoying the cooler heights during this time.

Tolis and Takis Kaloyannis
27522

Tolis and Takis – father and son? Marina feels her hope reignited at the sight of his name.

She has brought no bag and so no phone. However, her legs feel energised as if the years of sitting in her shop have stored up the need to move. The thought of the walk up into the mountains gives her a thrill. Before the muscles in her calves have had a chance to relax, she strides out again along the path and turns to cut down the side of the valley, and then left to head further along the island through the pine woods. She leaves behind houses that look as if they have not been lived in for years, and even some that, when viewed from the rear, prove to be no more than shells, their roofs fallen in long ago. Another cockerel calls as the pine trees close behind Marina, muffling all sound.

Marina's lungs claw as the track begins to climb steeply now. She pauses to take breath and can see the streak of sun between the pine trees stretching across the sea. The hill on the far side of the boatyard behind her shades the pine trees from the dawn, and the needled undergrowth is still, quiet and dark. The path continues, and after some time Marina wonders if she will gain the mountain village before the sun forces her to hastily retreat. The path turns further inland and, as she tops one hill, another hill even higher appears. It seems too far. There is a mountainous ridge to her right and a rocky outcrop to her left. It keeps the path in the shade. The sun has not yet risen here. Marina feels sure she can make it to the top of the next hill, but what if there is yet another hill beyond that?

She decides the top of the next hill is her turning point. But as this is gained and she deliberates at which tree exactly she will turn and admit defeat, she sees a very long-eared hare leap across the road above her, its black tufted ears so comical. Marina wishes to see another and climbs some more in hope, and is rewarded. The hare pauses, squatting on hind legs, front legs dangling, tufted ears upright, swivelling. She giggles and stays alert for more. The trees are thinning and the hare darts towards an open area. Marina follows the path, mesmerised.

She can hear a cockerel crow somewhere up the road and the trees have thinned out to scrub. Goat bells tell her she is not far from human habitation. Another cockerel. A walled enclosure. A donkey's saddle, wood and padded leather, by the side of the road. Marina's excitement grows as there on a hillock in front of her she sees the first mountain village house, this one flat-roofed, with low stone walls and mesh fences running below it to contain the cockerel and some hens, which run towards her excitedly.

The hill on her left still keeps the sun at bay, and as Marina passes the house on the hill the road divides, left into a dell with two cottages dotted, or right towards a two-storey stone house on a ridge that Marina feels sure will give her a view down the other side of the island.

The idea of seeing such a view appeals, and she turns right. Set into the hillside by the road is a big concrete tank, no doubt for water. Hanging by its feet, from one corner of the block, is a seagull, its beak open, its tongue protruding, its eyes crusted white. Marina recoils.

People come here to hunt. Rabbits and hares in the summer. The place suddenly feels sinister and Marina turns to retrace her steps. It is then that she sees the village. It is not the one or two houses she has seen. Here, on this side of the flat-roofed house, are a dozen houses all crowded in together in the shade of the hillock.

Instead of there being four houses for Marina to check, there are twenty. Finding a single man's house without causing undue interest will not be possible. Marina gasps. What if he is not single? What if he is married, and Eleni is 'the other woman'? Marina crosses herself twice and pushes the thought away. But the thought will not dissipate. It explains Eleni's reticence, her anger.

'Oh, my poor baby,' she says to the sky, and sinks down to sit on a wall.

'Who's your poor baby?'

Marina jolts. The chickens have spoken. She turns her head to see which chicken it is. An angelic boy smiles back up at her. He is crouched on the ground with his hand open, resting on the floor. The hens pick corn from his upturned palm. He is wearing a pair of swimming trunks. His feet are black, his dark tan even, his hair sticking out at every angle, messy from sleep. He obviously lives in his shorts. Red shorts. He is as blonde as the gods themselves. His eyes brown, dark brown. Marina is dazzled.

'This one is *my* baby,' he says, and picks up a fluffy-bottomed red Rhode Island hen. The chicken seems very happy tucked under his arm. He fishes in a home-made bag slung over his shoulder and holds out a handful of corn to her. She pecks eagerly.

'She's beautiful,' Marina says

'Who are you up here to see?'

'Oh! I am not sure, maybe no one.'

'A long way to come to see no one.'

He struts about the enclosure with the hen under his arm. Marina stands to leave.

'Are you going?'

'I suppose. You don't have any water, do you?'

The boy drops the hen and shuffles through the gate of the enclosure, ensuring it closes behind him. Marina presumes he has a bottle of water on the other side but instead he runs away, the soles of his feet like white rabbit tails behind him, his blonde mop streaming.

'See you, chickens,' Marina says, and, pushing her weight forward, rises slowly and begins to walk away. She cannot think how to carry out her mountaintop task. She cannot knock door to door with any discretion and she can think of no other way of finding who lives where. In the dimness of her mind a cloud of misery folds over her.

'I probably just haven't had enough sleep,' she says to the cockerel.

'My dad says I should sleep longer in the afternoon but I never do.'

Marina only twitches this time. 'Don't do that!'

'Do you still want this?' The boy holds out a bottle of water, frosted over with cold. Marina takes it and drinks deeply. It spills down her dress but she doesn't care. The sun isn't over the highest hill yet but the air is warming. Everything will dry within minutes soon enough.

'Are you going back down?'

'Yes.'

'Can I come? I'm allowed as far as the first corner, by the fallen pine.'

Marina smiles her reply, and they begin at his pace: slow, stone-kicking, no time limits. He is not more than six, seven, maybe a small eight. It has been too long for Marina. Her family grown, she cannot judge children's ages any more. She must look like an old granny to him. Actually, maybe not, now she is in a blue dress. She feels younger in it.

'Who says you can go as far as the fallen pine tree?'

'My mum. Vikki's not even allowed to the hen coop but she is only five. But that's in the summer. In the winter we are allowed as far up the road as the pine trees and the other way just to the beach, not along the coastal path.'

He picks up a stone and throws it at an olive tree. It ricochets into a bush and something scuttles away.

'That's if I am at the boatyard. But since I started school I lived last winter with an aunt in town so I could go to lessons every day.'

'Is Vikki your sister?'

The boy stops and darts off the path and returns with a tortoise. It is a large old one. He puts it on the road heading the way they are going and begins to walk with steps so small he is keeping pace with it. Marina stops walking and looks around her to gauge the sun's progress. She is still holding the bottle and drinks again.

'Can I have some?' Marina hands him the bottle. He drinks and pours some on his head – an action copied from an elder – and gives the bottle back. 'She's my cousin. We live in the same house at the boatyard in the winter when our dads are working, but in the summer we live next door.'

'So you are a Kaloyannis?'

'Yes, Dimi. What's your name?'

Marina thinks to withhold it. What if Eleni is his dad's secret lover? It could get too complex for Marina to think through.

'What's your dad's name?'

'Dad.'

'And your uncle's name?'

173

'Uncle Toli. He's great. He lets me climb up his front, over his shoulders and down his back, and then through his legs without touching the ground.'

Tolis Kaloyannis! Marina crosses herself and thanks the mother of Jesus for all her help. She smiles from ear to ear and ruffles his hair. He pulls his head away sharply and smooths a hand over his scalp. He takes a step away from her and pinches his mouth closed, his movements subdued.

'Big guy, is he?'

Hair-ruffling forgotten, his limbs take on new life and he turns and runs backward a little as he explains with his hands just how big Uncle Toli is.

'He is a giant! Nearly as big as Dad,' he concludes. 'I have seen him pull a rowing boat into the yard by himself! Once when a boat in the yard was being held up by sticks it started to topple, and he held it up until my dad found more sticks. But he scared me then. He shouted so loudly at me.'

'Shouted at you?'

'Get out of the way!' Dimi bellows in the lowest pitch he can manage. 'Oh, there's the pine tree.'

Marina stops her slow walk to turn to her companion, but he has turned already and is walking away. He looks back and calls, 'Who did you say you came up here to see again?'

'I think I came up here to see you!'

Dimi grins and waves, before taking off at a run.

The journey down from the fallen pine to the boatyard seems so swift, but as Marina comes out of

174

the pine forest and enters the boatyard's valley she can see the sun is peeking over the high hill, so she knows the coastal path will be basking without shade in the morning sun. It is already hot. Marina finishes the bottle of water.

The houses with roofs that she thought were uninhabited in the basin behind the boatyard have their shutters open. Near the road there, a man scoops water from a large blue-painted barrel, bucket by bucket. Tree by tree, he waters young olives. He calls a cheery 'Good morning!' as Marina passes and waves his bucket in salute.

Even the boatyard house with the arch has one shutter open, and the slight breeze brings the smell of old leather, wood and polish.

But still the boats in the yard lie untended, the only life that of the small chugging fishing boat which is now skimming around the outside of the bay with one man on board, trailing a line. The cockerel is still crowing, and the sun lights up one half of the valley. Soon the valley will be thick with heat, holding in the warmth until the evening.

Marina turns out of the shade onto the coastal path, and the heat of the sun hits her. From dawn to full heat in a single step. She pulls her hat down so the brim hides her face and, looking down at her feet, marches for home.

The loose thread she spotted earlier on the toe of her shoe has now worked its way into a loop, and the leather that it was securing shows the smallest gap. The black butterflies have increased in number and sit still on the path until her footsteps approach, and then they flit and weave around each other, pairing off in circles of courtship.

The heat on this stretch of the journey is weak compared to her expectation. She estimates it is still only about seven thirty, maybe eight. A firm pace brings her to the cluster of houses where she finds a rarely used bin for her water bottle. Fresh donkey manure on the road tells her that for some work has begun. The butterflies seem to relish their warm early-morning breakfast.

She takes the back road that she came by, back to Zoe's house. One or two people wish her a good day as they sweep their front steps, water their vegetable patches or sit for the first moments of their day: men with the eternal cigarette, woman in plain black dresses and headscarves.

Marina's legs are tiring, and she keeps her head down as Eleni could be around any corner. The spillage from when she drank out of the bottle has left a water mark on her dress and her shoe now has a hole, her sock clearly visible. The thought of lying down back in her room appeals strongly.

The stairs up to her door are almost too much, and Marina pushes her hands on her knees to lever herself up the last few.

The clock by her bed says eight thirty as she steps quietly into her room, her day's work already done and with no chance of bumping into Eleni. She is pleased. As she pulls off her shoes the hole becomes bigger. Marina sticks her finger through it from the

176

inside and wonders if she can stitch it. She is too tired to care, and stuffs her socks in her shoes, one in each, and throws them in the corner. Just before succumbing to the lure of her mattress she takes out her piece of paper and puts a line through Apostolis Kaloyannis's name. She feels smug at her cunning ability to cross him off without even having met him.

Two names to go, Socrates Rappas and Alexandros Mavromatis, and then, no matter what the outcome, she must think of her own needs. She is aware that her care for Eleni is acting as a smothering blanket over the emotions of her own that she must face before leaving the island. She must deal with the pain of all those years ago. She closes her eyes. There is an owl hooting outside the window even though the day is now well established.

Chapter 13

'*Ela, ela, pame.*' Come on, let's go, someone is shouting. Doors bang. Marina hovers on the edge of sleep trying to make sense of the noises; which are dreams and which reality?

Many voices all talking at once.

'Calm down, how do you know?'

'I had a call and now the line is dead. Please come, hurry.'

'Roula, I have to go.' It is Zoe's voice. Marina can hear Roula crying. Sleep dispelled, Marina rolls off the bed and pushes on her flip-flops.

'What's happening? Can I help?' Marina stumbles out to the balcony, rubs sleep from her slack face. She tries to straighten her hair. There is a strong wind blowing. It feels cooling. Marina relaxes in its gentle kiss.

'I have to go now, please.' Irini's eyes are wide, her body twitching. Signs of panic.

'What's wrong?' Marina puts a calming hand on Irini's shoulder. She tries to still her with her hand's pressure.

'Irini's fiancé called. He said he hit some rough water. Now his line is dead.' Zoe is hugging Roula, who is crying. Her eyes reflect the raised tension. 'She called one of the other taxi boats. They say his VHF radio is also dead.' Roula wails. Zoe tries to encompass her in her arms.

'Marina, come with me?' Irini asks, her voice trembling.

'Yes, of course, my dear. Where?'

'Port police. Get them to go and find him. I was about to go but…' Zoe looks down at Roula, whose head is against her chest. She is stroking her hair.

Irini takes Marina by the arm. Marina is all but pulled down the steps and out onto the street. They are on the path to town before Marina comes to her senses and realises she has forgotten her bag and her hat. But neither hat nor bag seems important. Marina releases her mind from the thoughts of Irini's fiancé and realises she has just agreed to walk right into the place she needs to avoid the most. Port police. Eleni.

They enter the harbour area. Irini begins to ask people where the port police are. Marina wonders what the date is. Has her daughter begun working yet? If she hasn't, will the port police want to take her name? Can she avoid going in?

'Irini,' Marina begins. She cannot go into the port police office.

'Look, all the other boats are in.' Irini points at the taxi boats and begins to cry, and walks faster. The wind is whipping round the port. The cats huddle in shop doorways. The waiters are inside. The outdoor tables have been cleared of napkins, glasses and menus. The sky is darkening. A donkey on the corner begins its loud sad bray. It echoes. The town feels empty.

Irini runs ahead and stops a man who is getting off one of the taxi boats. He turns his back to the wind as he talks to her, his chin tucked in and shoulders hunched. His words are whisked away from Marina by the wind. When she catches up with Irini she sees her face is wet with tears. The man slopes off to a café.

'He says all the other radios are still working. The port police are just here.' Irini turns to a door between two shops. A small white sign outside, no bigger than a postcard, declares its importance.

'Irini, I...' Marina begins again, but Irini's frightened tear-stained face shows more sorrow than she can bear. Marina closes her mouth and allows herself to be pulled into the port police office. After all, she now recalls, Eleni is not due to start for another couple of weeks.

There is no one behind the desk. Marina looks around for a newspaper to hide her face, just in case. The room is sparse, blue-and-white-themed, with a coffee table and one wooden rush-seated chair. The walls are decorated with damp-buckled prints of stormy seas behind dirty glass in thin frames. Judging by the countertop, which is painted a sharp blue, Marina can tell it has not been decorated since the seventies, and that even then it was done on a budget.

Irini is tapping impatiently on the counter. From somewhere in the depths, through another door, they can hear someone on a fizzing radio declaring *apagoreftiko*, a shipping ban due to high winds. The severity of the situation sinks in. Marina looks at Irini. She is tapping for attention with renewed persistence, her mouth a thin line of self-control. Marina takes a step towards her. She gently puts an arm around her.

'He has only been using the boat this year. He doesn't know much.' Irini stops tapping and falls into Marina's arms, crying. Marina holds her as if she is her own, stroking and kissing her hair, soothing her noises. She clucks and cuddles and becomes lost in the action.

A clicking of hobnailed boots approaches. Someone has come in through the door behind the counter. Marina looks up with a start.

For a split second there is a loaded silence.

Eleni has her hair tied back under her black cap. Wide-eyed, she spots her mother, her mouth hard. Marina loosens her grip around Irini.

In the same second Irini turns and pulls away from Marina. With her hands on the counter she shouts through her tears.

'Petta's on the boat *Hera*. He's missing. Dead radio. End of the island.'

Eleni drags her stare from her mother's face, quickly taking in her blue dress.

Marina can feel her cheeks are red. But her attention is jolted. *Hera*.

'Petta? *Hera*? The dancing man?' Marina demands. Eleni turns back to her.

Irini ignores her. Time slows, allowing Marina to think.

She pieces it together. Irini saying he wasn't there when looking at the taxi boats. The conversation she had with the boatman when he said he had only been on the boat a year, and Irini's statement that he has only been using the boat this year. Both have said they were engaged. Marina puts it all together.

'Panayia. Mother of God, keep him safe.' She crosses herself three times and kisses the cross hanging around her neck.

Eleni, who is still looking at her, now appears puzzled and opens her mouth to finally speak. Irini slams her fist down on the counter.

'Now!' she demands.

A man comes rushing through the door behind Eleni.

'We've had a Mayday on the radio. End of the island. VHF intermittent, no mobile. We are the nearest boat. Come on, we're off.'

He shoves Eleni out from behind the counter in front of him. Irini is shouting for them to hurry. Marina makes a prayer for the dancing captain. Concern at being spotted by Eleni is lost in the greater worry over her friend's life.

Irini runs out after them.

The skies are even darker. The water is choppy even in the harbour. Lines slap noisily against the masts and the wind hums through the metal stays of the yachts. Out in the bay the waves are white-capped, the mainland opposite a menacing black outline.

Four port police are running ahead of Marina to their boat. Irini is in their way, and a big port policeman lifts her bodily to one side. Marina hurries her steps and puts an arm around her as the port police boat casts off.

Eleni is coiling ropes at the back of the boat and, as the tail end passes Marina, she shouts above the wind, 'Stay safe.' Eleni's look freezes her. Irini turns to Marina and cries, as if the event has reached an inevitable conclusion already. Marina wraps her arms around Irini, comforting herself as much as the little waif.

Chapter 14

Eleni piles the ropes on the stern seat.

'Don't leave them there, put them in the locker,' the captain shouts, looking over his shoulder at her.

Eleni lugs the ropes to the deck and lifts up the seat that doubles as a cover for the rope locker. The sea is jolting the boat hard. She broadens her stance. The locker lid slams down with the jar of a wave. She takes the impact on her arm, cursing herself for not putting on the safety latch. She pulls her arm free and allows the lid to slam home. She rubs at the pain as another wave takes her balance.

'Come inside,' a voice shouts above the noise of the engine. It's Spiros.

Eleni staggers towards the cabin and unhooks a clipboard from above the chart table, and grabs the pen swinging on a length of string to note the time of their departure. She leans against the door frame. The cabin is open at the rear and the engine noise drowns the crew's voices. The radio crackles with indistinct words.

The boat gathers speed until its bows are smashing against the waves, rising and falling with power and urgency. The captain stands, thighs braced against the dashboard, looking out into the grey. It has begun to rain.

The other two men are sitting, one each side of the boat, on long benches. One, Spiros, is trying to smoke but the spasmodic movement makes him miss his mouth when he raises the cigarette to his lips.

Eleni returns the clipboard to its hook and allows the pen on the string to drop. This is her first rescue trip. She looks back to see if her mother is still standing on the quay, but they have already turned out of the port and round the first headland. It is not just that Mother is on the island, but that she walked straight into the port police office. In a blue dress. Hugging a stranger. Praying for a taxi boat man.

'You OK?' Spiros, with a half-smoked cigarette, shouts and moves along the bench, indicating that she should sit. Eleni nods and staggers across to the seat. They pass the two small islands topped with tiny whitewashed churches. The islands are menacing black rocks in the stormy half-light, white water foaming. Now they are drawing level with the boatyard.

If her mother is on the island interfering with her life, what has that got to do with her no longer being in mourning dress? Blue, for goodness' sake. It actually suits her, but pale blue is a long way from black. Why not brown, or even navy?

'Do you feel sick?' He flicks his cigarette to the rear opening, a practised action, confident that the wind will take the glowing end into the sea.

'No, I am fine.' Eleni wipes her cheek. She is not sure if it is tears or spray. Her stomach turned and sank at seeing her mother's arms around another girl, a stranger. Who is she? More importantly, who is she to her mother? Her stomach turns again at the thought. She would have liked to have been in those arms. She hasn't hugged her mother in how long? She wipes her cheek again.

The captain turns and scans the three of them before shouting. 'Come on, guys! Life jackets on!' The radio hisses and he picks it up and shouts for a repeat of the message.

Eleni reaches under her seat and pulls out a life jacket, and deftly hooks it over her head and ties it on. The other two sit unmoved. Spiros offers a cigarette.

Why did Mum cross herself when she realised who was missing? 'Dancing man', she called him. What does that mean? But if she was coming to report him missing, why was she so surprised when she found out who it was? It doesn't make sense. The vision of her on the dock holding the girl comes again. Eleni feels very alone.

The captain turns the radio to full volume. 'Boat...nd...isl ...ne ...ock.'

'Repeat, please, repeat!' the captain shouts. They are coming to the end of the island and no sighting is called by the captain. The waves tower here as the shelter of the channel gives way to open seas.

'Shi...ck...shi...ck.'

The captain turns to his men. 'Anyone understand that?'

The man opposite Eleni edges up his bench, towards the captain, away from the spray. Eleni doesn't know the area but she has heard stories. 'Maybe he meant "Ship Rock",' she ventures.

The captain presses the send button on his handheld VHF. The wind is tossing the boat from side to side and the force of the engine is ploughing them forward through unbroken waves, banging the bow down in the troughs and rearing them up like a cork on the crests.

Eleni begins to feel a little nervous.

'Did you say "Ship Rock"? Over.' The static increases but they all hear the reply: *nai* – yes. Spiros takes out another cigarette.

When Eleni arrived on the island and was introduced to her colleagues, they teased her about various things, breaking the ice, introducing themselves, flirting. But the stories of Ship Rock were told straight-faced. It is a jag of rock that comes straight out of the sea, reaching for the skies. From a distance it looks like a ship, a triangle of full sail. It is not far offshore, and sailors unfamiliar with the seas, believing it is a vessel, may sail near the coast, thinking it must be deep enough to pass. But the rock lifts its toes under the water and the sharp edges rip holes in the poor sailors' keels. If they are seaward when they sink, the current will take a man into open waters. There he must hope he is spotted, his tiny black head bobbing on a vast ocean of reflective, darkening wave. If he goes down between Ship Rock and the island there is a chance to swim to shore in calm weather. But, with wind and wave, craggy teeth await a man there, the sharpened incisors ripping muscles and limbs with each unforgiving swell, making breakfast for crabs.

Eleni stands to gauge their position. She clings to the overhead handrail and allows her body to swing with the motion. They have rounded the end of the island. The wipers, on full power, allow snatches of vision. She can see the 'sail' of Ship Rock, black against the grey sky.

Does her mother have a whole other life she does not know about? Has she found out her own secret? Maybe it would be better if she has. The vision of her hand stroking the girl's hair makes Eleni's stomach churn. She sits down again.

'Feeling sick?' Spiros flicks another cigarette end past her, out to the deep.

Eleni is about to reply that she is, but reflects that it is not the movement of the boat that is disturbing her. She shakes her head.

'You look like you have swallowed a bad fish.'

'There!' the captain shouts, and all three crew jump up to view the job in hand.

The taxi boat is between Ship Rock and the island. The swell is causing it to wallow about to such a degree that it is difficult to make out if there is anyone on board.

Eleni wonders again why her mother called him dancing man.

The water appears black here. In the channel, little frills of white suggest unseen rocks lurking just beneath the heaving surface. Ship Rock's face to their right rears smooth, glistening with spray, belying the rasps hidden under its skirt of black silk and white lace. The island to the left is jagged and split, with dark scars and gashes that run vertically from the churning froth.

'*Hera*, can you hear me? Over.' The captain puts the boat into neutral. They are a good enough distance away not to be carried into the channel by the current. The radio crackles no reply.

'*Hera*, answer please.' The static has no voice within it.

'There!' Eleni cries. She points to the rear of the taxi boat where for a second a man appears, before diving into the water. The captain leans over his dashboard and peers between the wipers.

'Mother of God.' He crosses himself. 'What is he doing?' He crosses himself again and kisses the cross around his neck. Eleni mutters under her breath her love for her mother.

Spiros grabs the binoculars swinging from their peg. He marches to the stern of the boat to look out unimpeded by the boat's salty windows.

Eleni searches the waves, the silver shards of reflection distracting from her search for the dark spot of the man's head. The captain pushes past her. Eleni thinks she sees the man but another wave rolls in and her vision is broken.

With a snap the captain turns on the searchlight. Its beam lights the whole channel. Eleni sees the man. 'There,' she shouts, pointing, but the captain on deck cannot hear her. The man at the helm, second in command, pushes her behind him to indicate she should go on deck to tell the captain.

On deck the whole thing feels more real. The wind grabs handfuls of foam and hurls them at her. The sea around the port police boat swirls and rises, fingers of foam reaching over the deck, feeling for prey. Eleni clings to the handrail and goes forward. The rain and the sea fill her senses, blocking her ears, pitting her skin, thrilling her soul.

She pulls on the captain's sleeve and points. He sees the man.

The taxi boat man is swimming hard, following a line. The boat is roped to a large rock some distance from the island, surrounded by serrated teeth. It is hard to tell which is wave and which is rock. The head is gone, the line dips. A wave rears and the head reappears. Eleni gasps. The captain swears. He's gone again. The rain stops but the relentless pounding continues. He is there again, his arms pulling hard, halfway to the rock. 'Mother of God,' the captain prays.

'What do we do?' Eleni shouts.

'Nothing. If we go towards him we will either hit the rocks or his boat will hit us.'

'We have to do something.'

He's gone again. A large wave, the line taut. His boat strains on the line and he reappears, close to the rock. He stops swimming and backstrokes, a metre or so from the rock. The waves crash and suck back. The man's arms are outstretched. He treads water and a wave lifts him. He lurches into a crawl. The wave rises, the man on top. Tears prick Eleni's eyes. She closes them; he will be smashed. 'Mother of God,' the captain exhales. Eleni opens her eyes. The man is clinging to the rock. The sea sucks back. He climbs higher, the sea pulling at his feet. He pauses at the line holding his boat.

'What's he doing?' Eleni shouts.

'If he has any sense he will be cutting his boat free. We have a chance of getting to him.'

'Captain, he's cutting it free,' Spiros, with the binoculars, calls from the stern. The captain turns. Eleni follows the cue. Hand over hand, they return from the prow into the cabin. The captain takes the helm from the first mate. He puts the craft into reverse.

'The line's free,' Spiros calls.

The taxi boat nods in agreement. It rears with the next wave and comes hurtling out of the channel straight at them. The captain slams into forward gear and spins the boat off to one side. The crewless taxi boat sails past. The initial momentum dissipates as it floats off to sea.

'Right, to work!' the captain shouts.

The second in command takes ropes and life rings from the stern lockers. He doesn't put the safety latch on either, and the lid slams into his arm. He doesn't flinch. The captain calls them round him.

191

'We are going out there.' He points to the right of Ship Rock. 'We are then going to turn towards the island and pass straight in front of Ship Rock. There are no underwater hazards there. When we are bridging the channel we are going to swing around. Our stern will go into the channel and we will be pointing out to sea. The arc of our turn will give you a chance to throw a life ring to our friend out there, and if the rocks don't get him we will. OK?'

'*Nai.*' They chorus their understanding.

The three crew ready themselves and the captain thrusts the throttle forward, taking them away from the booming channel into the rolling swells of the sea. It sounds alarmingly quiet by comparison. Eleni decides that if she has the courage to get through this she will tell her mother everything. Then she will see if her mother still loves her, if she will hug her the way she hugged that girl.

'On deck,' the captain commands, and turns the boat to make their attempt.

The crew of three wait in the stern of the boat. Ship Rock towers past them on their right, the indistinct darkness of its surface like a shadow bringing death. Cold. Close. Eleni shivers.

The bow clears the rock and points across to the island. Then the cacophony of the narrow channel grasps all thoughts and hurls them to the wind. Eleni's hat is whipped from her head and some of her hair escapes her ponytail. It lashes her across her eyes. The wind blows her shirtsleeves into balloons. She holds the handrail tighter with one hand and

192

readies the life ring in the other, ready to throw with all her might.

'Ready,' the captain shouts. He spins the helm and the boat turns with acute sharpness, the stern spinning into the channel. There is a deep grating sound. The vessel shudders. Eleni can feel the deck vibrate with the sound. She holds her breath. The rocks grind beneath the hull. Spiros throws his life ring but the wind takes it too far to the left. The boat swings round further. The grating judders the deck more, and then ceases. The second in command throws his life ring at the same time as Eleni. The man on the rock, now only yards away, catches one but loses his grip. It slides down his chest. Clinging to the rock, he sticks out his foot. The ring lodges. Holding on to the rock with one hand he bends to lift the ring from his foot.

Eleni has frozen. The wind buffets her against the handrail. She cannot see the possibility of his escape. He pulls the ring over his wide chest. He waits. The slack in the line is taken up as the captain eases the police boat forward. When it is taut the man on the rock readies himself. The captain is looking over his shoulder as he drives, watching the man. As the rope starts to pull, the man on the rock jumps. Eleni sees the rocks beneath him. She swallows hard. The captain edges the boat forward, a little too fast, and the line snaps taut, pulling both ring and man forward with a jerk as they sail through the air. He lands in the dark. The captain eases the speed back.

The engine strains at slow revs against the wind. Eleni cannot see the man.

The crew are silent. Watching. The wind howls, the noise of the channel booming. The engine throbs.

'There!' they all shout in close unison. A dark shape and an orange ring bob to the surface. The crew rush to winch in the line, hand over hand. The captain keeps the vessel steady.

The second in command and Spiros jump down onto the step below the back of the boat. The man appears lifeless, his arm hooked through the orange ring. His shirt is torn and Eleni can see blood on his skin. They haul him into the boat and for a moment they stand around him, exhausted. Eleni snaps into action first and feels for a pulse. The captain, seeing he is aboard, throttles forward and heads for the harbour at full speed.

'He's alive.' Eleni smiles up at the other crew members. The man coughs violently and rolls onto his back, and opens his eyes.

'Of course I am alive!' he coughs again. 'And I will dance at my wedding!'

The dancing man. Eleni likes his smile. It seems familiar.

'What is your name?' the captain asks.

'They call me Petalouda – the butterfly.'

'A name well deserved, my friend,' Spiros teases as he recognises him. 'You flitted from girl to girl all your life, like a butterfly from flower to flower.'

'Petta for short,' he tells Eleni. He coughs again and tries to sit up. He winces and lifts the collar of his shirt to look at his shoulder. 'Huh! The island bit me! What took you guys so long?'

Eleni takes the first-aid box from above the chart table and crouches down to unbutton his shirt. The gashes in his shoulder are jagged and deep but they are not bleeding profusely. She presses a pad of gauze over them and begins to bandage him.

'Captain, can you do me a favour?' Petta tries to turn to the captain, who nods. 'Can you call Petro at the taxi boats and see if he can go pick up the boat?' Petta turns to Eleni. 'Not my boat – I will wish I had died back there if I don't return it.' He laughs heartily until he winces.

The skies are lightening but the wind is not dropping. The police boat tosses and ploughs back past the boatyard, level with the two rock islands topped with churches. The crew cross themselves as they pass. Eleni reaffirms the decision to tell her mum her secret; they have been apart too long. Time to reclaim her mother or mourn her loss.

'One minute you're safe, the next you are nearly dead!' Petta exclaims, grinning.

Eleni decides to tell her mother as soon as they get back to shore.

'Yeah, what happened out there, buddy?' Spiros offers Petta a cigarette. He takes it casually and Eleni starts to coil the ropes attached to the life rings. One has fallen down on the step behind the boat. It has become stuck. She leans over to release it.

'I had just dropped some tourists on the beach at the back of the island. Oh my goodness, they will still be there! Captain, can you call a taxi boat to pick them up?'

The ring will not come free. Eleni puts a leg over the rail, a hobnailed boot on the step. The spray blinds her. The propeller churns the sea. The wind changes direction, snatching Petta's words away. She reaches for the ring, pulls on the rope to free it. It is fast. She wraps the rope around her wrist for grip. The wind changes again. Petta's tale is accompanied with the spray.

'Engine just cut. But when I tried to restart it the battery was flat...'

Eleni straddles the handrail. She uses both hands to pull the rope. The boat wallows and rears. Coils of rope fall into the sea. Eleni sees the danger. Releases the rope. It is caught round her wrist. The propeller takes the rope, sucking it under. Coiled around its shaft, grinding. Hauling it down, twisting, cutting. Eleni's breath quickens. She scrabbles to release her hand. The slack is all but gone. The propeller draws all attached to it to the deep. She will be pulled under. Shredded. Drowned.

'I tied it to the rock when all was calm...' Petta draws deeply on his cigarette. He is still on the floor. He looks up to Spiros and then beyond. He jerks up to sitting. Spiros follows his gaze. A leg and a hobnailed boot. The wind and engine too loud. A silent splash.

'Man overboard!' Spiros yells, jumping to his feet and throwing his butt end into the sea. He leaps to the handrail. 'Cut the engine!'

'What!' The captain is aware that cutting the engine in such conditions means losing his control to the sea. But no sooner has the word left his mouth than he can hear the propeller whining. Then screaming. The engine dies. They are adrift.

The second in command has the rope around a winch in seconds. They wind it into the boat, at first with great effort. Spiros joins in, hoping Eleni is on the end of it. A frayed end shoots into the boat.

'Mother of God, where's the girl?' the captain bellows. Spiros points to the stern. The captain jumps over the sprawled men. He is over the handrail, onto the step. He searches the sea. The second in command is on his feet, life ring in hand. 'There.' He points. She is face down.

'Drop an anchor,' yells the captain, and dives over the side. He pulls through the water with ease, his life jacket buoyant in the heaving, breathing brine. He grabs at her. Draws her closer. Flips her onto her back. Wet hair straggles her face. Her eyes are closed. The life ring is thrown, and the rope attached is clipped to her buoyancy jacket. Eleni and the captain are hauled to the craft.

With one hand Spiros pulls her into the cockpit and checks for a pulse. The captain climbs aboard. He coughs and heaves for air before he and the second in command turn their attention to the rope around the propeller. No propeller means no engine. The wind is still strong and they have drifted nearer the island. The gusts are broken by the rise of land. The edge is rocky all the way along, with nowhere they can safely land. The boat rocks, the movement no longer harsh.

'Why are we drifting? Check the anchor,' the captain shrieks. The second in command looks at Spiros, who is turning Eleni's head to one side to clear her airways of water.

'You didn't drop a bloody anchor! Are you simple? Panayia! Drop it, drop it now,' the captain shouts into the second in command's face.

Water pours from Eleni's nose and mouth. Spiros straightens her head to begin artificial resuscitation. Petta looks on, his shoulder bleeding through the gauze and bandage.

The captain has a knife between his teeth. A rope round his waist is tied to the handrail. He must cut the rope from the propeller. He removes his life jacket, slips into the sea, one hand on the step, head under water. He lets go. The swirling black encloses him. He is back within seconds.

'Too dark,' he yells to the wind. He pulls himself aboard. Spiros lifts his head from Eleni, who arches her back and coughs, spraying him with water. The captain strides over her to the VHF.

Chapter 15

'This is port police vessel KA66172. Repeat, port police Kappa Alpha 66172. Can anyone hear me? Vasilli, are you there? Stamo, are you around?'

'The anchor's not holding, sir.'

'Did you give it enough line?'

'All we've got.'

'Vasilli, Stamo, anyone there?'

'Shall I try the boatyard, sir? Tolis listens in on channel 20.'

The captain shakes his head and tuts. 'He's up in the mountains this time of year.'

'Worth a try though, sir. He does go down and tinker in the boatyard sometimes.'

'Toli, are you there? This is port police KA66172.'

Eleni is coughing and trying to sit up. Petta, despite his bleeding shoulder, is trying to assist her. Spiros lights a cigarette. The VHF crackles. The wind seems to be dropping.

'There's no answer, sir.'

'Try again.'

'Toli, are you there? Toli?' The line crackles.

'Forget it,' the captain says.

The island is a wall of rock. They are close enough to see where birds have nested. The water is crashing around the base, black and ominous, with white foam on top.

'Eh? Is that you, *kapetanio*?' The crackling line becomes clearer. The captain grabs the radio, and smiles at the sound of Tolis's voice and his use of the official title, despite the fact that they grew up together.

'Toli, you lazy rat, can you pull yourself away from your fancy satellite television and give an old friend a hand?'

'Couldn't possibly. I'm just about to watch the match. What's your trouble, my friend?' The captain smiles and his frown relaxes.

'The rookie got a rope around the prop. Cut the engine, just past your yard. Drifting to the rocks.' His frown is back.

'Is that all? I thought it must be serious, what with you calling me by name, personal, like. It will take me about an hour and a half to get to you if I watch the match first, or I could be there in five or ten minutes if I hurry.'

'Right then, see you in an hour and a half, you lazy rat.' The captain is grinning but the line is already dead. Tolis is on his way. The captain kisses the evil eye pendant around his neck and tells his crew they are such a bad lot that they have the luck of the devil. The captain turns. Eleni's head is resting back against the seat locker. Petta has his eyes closed. The second in command is at the bows trying to secure a hold with the anchor and Spiros is standing next to him, one hand on the rail and the other holding a cigarette.

The captain breathes out heavily. He leans his weight against the dashboard to steady himself, lights a cigarette, then pulls a small silver flask from his pocket and takes a nip, followed by another, and another.

The wind is dropping. Eleni opens her eyes and focuses on the island. The storm seems to be passing as the sky has lightened, even though the sun is still masked by a layer of grey cloud. She watches the island a while longer. They are not motoring and yet they are moving. There is no thumping of the engine.

She turns to look at Petta sitting next to her. His shoulder is still bleeding and his eyes are closed.

'You asleep?' He doesn't answer.

She turns to look at the helm. The captain is swigging from a silver flask. Beyond him, standing on the bows, she can see Spiros and the second in command bent over the anchor chain.

She looks down at herself. She is wet. Then, like a tsunami, the memory of falling in the water engulfs her. Her breathing stops and her throat constricts until both give way to a sob. She puts a hand over her mouth to hide her emotion. She longs for her mother. To be held in her arms. To be young and safe again. To feel loved by her. To not have the secret that drives them apart.

The sound of an engine can be heard. The captain pockets his flask.

'Ahoy, you pirates!'

'Ah, Toli. Now you come! What took you so long? It's been five minutes.'

'Close your mouth and open your fist and catch this.' A rope falls into the boat over Eleni's head. The captain steps over her legs to retrieve it and makes it fast on a cleat.

The crew return from the bows.

'So what do you want me to do, you old sea dog? Take you back to my boatyard and claim you as salvage, or tow you into the port to leave the islanders to make fun of your botched rescue?'

'That reminds me, Toli, I haven't seen your licence for some time now...'

'Ach! Licences are for mainlanders. So where shall we go?' The two men face each other, each captain of his own vessel. 'And before we go, give me a nip from that flask you keep attached to you!'

The captain slips out the flask and throws it across.

'You must have been scared, my friend! This is half empty!' He takes a hearty swig and tosses it back. 'Come on then. You'll need the rest of the day to do your paperwork.' Tolis laughs from his belly, all six feet of him shaking.

Spiros undoes the line from the rear cleat and walks it to the bows. The second in command is pulling up the anchor. Spiros ties the line to the bow cleat.

Eleni makes a move to stand but finds she has neither the energy nor the balance. She can feel her cheeks glowing. Until now she has always felt strong and sure in her uniform and hobnailed boats. Now she feels small and useless. She wonders if tangling the line in the propeller will affect her new position on the island. She knows she will be subject to much jesting, but her main concern is will it land her permanently behind a desk?

There is a jerk. Petta's head rolls to rest on the other side. Eleni looks up. The captain is at the helm, flask in hand. Spiros is smoking and the second in command is sitting looking blank. The boat begins to move. They are under way and soon they build some speed.

It takes no more than a few minutes before their speed is cut and they enter the harbour. The sun is peeking through the clouds over the hilltops above the town and a shaft of sunlight spreads glitter on the tiled roofs. Eleni feels exhausted and closes her eyes at the comforting thought of the proximity of solid ground.

Marina and Irini are wet through from the rain and the spray. They huddle in the doorway of a shop on the harbour. Marina's instincts put her in the way of the wind and spray to protect Irini as much as she can. Irini has not stopped crying, first loud and hysterical, now a continuous quiet sob.

When they hear the engine of a boat coming around the corner Irini jumps from the doorway and begins to run towards the sound, only to sink onto the wet flags when she sees it is a private boat.

Marina looks a little longer, to see the police patrol boat being towed behind. She helps Irini to her feet. Irini is no longer crying. She is still.

The rigging of the yachts moored in the harbour is no longer clattering and the hum of the wind through the stays has subsided. The clouds over the top of the island have parted even further and a shaft of light is descending on the town. Some of the cafés open their doors. Snippets of laughter can be heard and the breeze carries the smell of tobacco and coffee, beer and roasted tomatoes.

The stunted clock tower chimes the hour and Marina walks Irini nearer to the harbour edge.

A group of men come hurrying into the port carrying various pieces of equipment on their shoulders. When they draw level with Irini and Marina they put two long canvas rolls on the ground and open them out lengthways, snapping pieces together to make stretchers.

Irini's eyes widen and her mouth drops open.

'It means nothing,' Marina coos, but her own heart quickens its pace. She cannot believe that she has kept her secret from her children for so long, long enough to alienate Eleni. She has been foolish and selfish and she will tell Eleni all as soon as she returns. 'God, let her be safe.'

'Let them all be safe,' one of the stretcher-bearers says.

The stretcher-bearers and Marina all cross themselves. Irini, a generation younger, kisses the stone in a small band of gold on her ring finger.

The boats pull alongside. Ropes are thrown, and the stretcher-bearers tie them to bollards on the pier.

'*Geia sou*, Toli.' One stretcher-bearer greets the first captain. Marina takes a momentary interest. His boat has a sign with the boatyard number. *So this is the mountain boy's uncle, Tolis Kaloyannis.* It feels odd to Marina to know something about this man without him knowing her, as if she has invaded his privacy. She nods to him when he looks her way, and he returns the nod blankly.

A port policeman gets off the second boat, smoking. He turns and puts out a hand to steady a man who is being all but carried off. Irini squeals.

'Petta!'

'Irini, my love.'

'You are hurt.'

'It is nothing.' But his strength is failing him, and it takes little persuasion to get him on a stretcher. Irini holds his hand. It appears that the world has ceased to exist for them beyond their eye contact with each other.

Marina is all but laughing at the sight of them. Her relief eases the tension in her chest slightly. There is a commotion aboard the police boat and Marina turns her attention and looks for Eleni. She will tell her straight, with no introduction. She will just blurt it out and Eleni can do what she will.

A big man in uniform is carrying someone in his arms. Marina gasps. The person is small. She can see long wet chestnut hair. *Eleni!* She rushes towards her but the stretcher-bearers cross her path. The port police are surrounding Eleni, fussing.

'I'll be fine,' Marina can hear Eleni say, and she exhales.

'Just let the doctors check you over. Call it overtime!' the big man in police uniform says, as he takes a small silver flask from his pocket. 'Medicinal!' He offers it, but the stretcher-bearers have raised her and the port police walk by her side. She is encircled by people. For Eleni's sake, Marina decides her confession must wait.

Feeling bewildered by all the excitement, Marina remains on the harbour side as the commotion subsides. She needs a minute alone before she follows. The first stretcher has already turned onto the lane away from the port towards the hospital, the bearers treading carefully on the wet flagstones. Eleni and her entourage are not far behind. A cat joins her party, weaving between legs. The boats that were the centre of so much activity now bob abandoned in front of her. She scans the police boat, Eleni's world. She sees something black on a cleat, trapped by a rope holding a fender. Marina steps towards it, an idle interest, wishing to blank her mind from the swirling emotions within her. She releases the item to see it is a police cap. She turns it in her hands, looks inside it to see if it is lined. There is a label with Eleni's name written in capitals.

Marina takes in a sharp breath, her heart palpitates and her legs feel strangely weak. She clutches the cap to her mouth, holding back all sound. Her face contorts behind the rough serge. A soundless wail rises in the back of her throat, forbidden, unbidden, strangling her airways, pushed from a place deep within. Her eyes crease to slits, tears on her eyelashes distorting the port like prisms. Marina is terrified of all that is rising from within her. It feels like standing on the edge of a very deep abyss. Her hands begin to shake. Her daughter could have died today. How many years of bad relations have resulted from her suppressed feelings?

Clutching the hat, she hurries after the stretchers. Turning from the port, she can see them entering the hospital grounds. The sun is now out and the way is speckled with cats washing themselves and basking. Marina breaks into a trot and is reminded of the last time she ran. That was also for Eleni.

The sun has dried the steps up to the little hospital's entrance. The double doors stand open and Marina can smell disinfectant. There is a screen half folded in the middle of the high-ceilinged entrance hall for no apparent reason and a group of people stand, two of them in white coats, chatting and smoking. One has a styrofoam cup in her hand. They ignore her.

Gloss-painted grey doors, chipped and worn, lead off the entrance hall on both sides. The first one on the right opens to a sunny reception room. The desks are covered in papers, ashtrays full, and there is no one there. The next room on the right has two beds in it. Both are empty and stripped. The room is stark.

Marina negotiates her way through the hall between the talking people, the screen and a trolley of instruments that she didn't notice before. The first room on the left has two beds and Petta is lying on one, with his shirt off. A nurse is treating his wounds. Irini sees Marina and pulls her in.

'Well, well, if it isn't my Lady Peacock.' Petta smiles and holds out a hand in greeting. Marina takes it and he pulls her in to kiss her on each cheek, friendly but traditional. As she moves away a priest bustles in, black robes flying, book in hand, his tall black pork pie hat knocked to an angle. He straightens himself and tries to look solemn.

'Socrates Rappas, you old rogue, are you hoping I was dead? Need a bit of work, do you?'

Marina feels she recognises the name but can't quite place it. The priest starts to fiddle with his book.

'Stop fiddling, man, and speak up!' Petta teases gently. The words jog Marina's memory. He is one of the last two men on her list.

'I just came to see you were OK, my friend,' he all but whispers.

'What a friend you are! Take a seat.' He pats the bed. 'How is your good wife, and the babies?'

Marina mentally strikes him from her list and backs out of the room.

'Lady Peacock, where are you going? You flit in and out of my life but you never stay. You are more of a butterfly than me.'

'Petta, we are neighbours! I will come to see you when you are at home. I am staying at Zoe's.' Marina feels warmth towards him. Irini makes her promise. Petta asks her name and the priest gently shakes her hand, finger ends to finger ends, limply, quietly, formally.

The group of people in the corridor are gone. The styrofoam cup sits on the trolley with the stainless steel instruments, and cigarette ends float on the remains of the coffee. Marina pops her head around the next door, the last room. There is a screen across, just inside the door, hiding the bed from direct view. She can hear many voices.

Looking between the metal frame and the material of the screen, she can see the white-coated people and the port police, all, presumably, surrounding Eleni, whom she cannot see. Marina searches the faces. One, surely, is Eleni's lover. Someone comes in behind her and says 'Excuse me' as they pass. She doesn't have time to turn to see who it is until they are on the other side of the screen. It is Panos and his boyfriend and the girl who was so calm and serene when Marina saw her last. She is crying. Panos turns to the girl.

'She's OK, Anna!' He puts his arm around the elegant girl. 'Look, Eleni is fine.'

Marina is surprised, but more than that she is pleased. Such nice young people for Eleni to mix with.

The port police start to leave one by one, wishing Eleni well. Marina wonders if the one whom they are calling Spiros will stay. Is he her boyfriend? She hopes not. He is a heavy smoker.

Marina catches a glimpse of her daughter and her heart skips a beat. She is grateful that Eleni is alive, and she is eager to share her secret and feels the outcome can only be positive. She wills the people to leave so she can confide in her. The men in white coats amble out and now there is only Panos and his friends by Eleni's bed.

Marina wonders why her young man has not come to be by her side. Maybe it is the port police captain and they are keeping it separate from the professional side of their relationship, and that's why he was the first to bid her farewell.

Panos turns to leave as a nurse goes in. Marina does not want the complication of explaining why she is there. She needs to keep her courage up and not become distracted. She pulls the hall screen around the instrument trolley and hides behind it, lining up the sharp metal knives, trying to look official. Some of them are very sharp and some are ugly and mean-looking, with big screw handles or spatula blades. She feels slightly sick.

Panos and his boyfriend pass through the hall, talking and laughing. The blonde young man's hair is shorter than when she first saw him. They look happy.

Marina turns to go back to the room. The nurse is leaving and Eleni must be alone now. She takes a deep breath and steps straight through the door and around the screen.

She cannot understand what she sees. Her mouth falls open. She frowns. She dives back behind the screen.

She peeks through the gap. Eleni is half lying in bed. Standing over her is the young woman in her elegant linen trousers. The girl, Anna, has scooped Eleni in her arms and is kissing her with passion. Marina swallows. Visions of grandchildren evaporate, white weddings gone. Big manly sons-in-law to tower over her and make her feel safe and protected are banished. Her hopes implode and her imagined future shatters. Her stomach feels hollow and her temples are throbbing. The scene begins to swirl. Marina puts a hand on the wall to steady herself.

She backs out into the hall, turns, and hurries down the steps and out into the sunshine.

Chapter 16

The path outside the hospital is dirty. There is donkey manure down the centre. Cats sit around looking scruffy. The doors to people's homes are painted drab colours, or not painted at all. The weeds, where whitewashed walls and stone paths meet, are brown and wilting. The sky has cleared and the sun beats down relentlessly, burning everything to a crisp.

Marina gasps some air and hurries in the direction of Zoe's, wiping tears from her eyes. A paper bag scuttles past her on the slightest of breezes. Forward she marches, up through the town and across the top and down. Her hands brush her face as tears gather on her chin. The steps come in small groups on this path. She looks down at her feet. Her flip-flops look ridiculous. And whatever possessed her to buy this blue dress?

She reaches the top of the steps by Aunt Efi's apartment. What was Aunt Efi thinking? How wrong of her, how evil. And her father, who initiated Marina's move with his sister. They were evil, wicked, selfish. Marina searches for a swear word, an expletive to expel some feelings. Toads! Donkeys! Cockroaches!

Bloody cockroaches. To do such a thing to a child. Her mother had not agreed. She did not want the tearing apart of mother and child. Marina did not see her mother for nearly a year then. So lonely, so incredibly, heartbreakingly lonely. All for their own needs, her father's needs. Cockroach!

She hears what she thinks is a donkey beginning to bray, but as the sound does not crack to the lower tones she realises it is a human cry. An extreme sound like an animal in distress. Her mouth is open, her chest expanded; this human, gut-wrenching sound is her own. Shocked, she covers her mouth with both hands, her eyes wide in the fear of all that is rising within her. She wants to scream. Her past hurtles into the present and collides with her grim, isolated, projected future. Her youngest daughter, more like her father, gone to Athens, unable to have children, now talking of emigrating to America. Her eldest, Eleni, so like herself, embracing a future of secrets and discretion and no grandchildren. No grandson. No baby boy. Another wail builds in her chest.

Marina runs down the steps, the jarring movement hiding her sobbing from herself, her mind wrapped in the thought that she will never hold that baby boy. She passes Irini's house and the other houses on the corner and takes the short path down to Zoe's.

Eleni is in a lifeless, fruitless relationship that will bring no joy, only gossip and shame in the eyes of God. And no babies.

Even Zoe's house looks drab. The tiles on the steps look old-fashioned, fussy, the pots of plants dried and lifeless, the flowers fake and displaced. She can hear Roula and Bobby talking above the television. *What's the point?* Marina feels how cruel life has been, and not only to her. Bobby, Roula, Zoe and Zoe's mother all have the vile twisted mark of life upon then. Just as she does. They all cope. But for what? Where's the reason, the rhyme? The joy?

Marina closes her door securely behind her. The room feels like a cell, her neatly made bed part of the regimentation of life, automatic, pointless. She flops onto the bed. All of it is pointless. Her being here is pointless. Her bag is on the floor but her list is by her bed. She grabs the list and screws it up tighter than necessary and throws it towards the bin by the window.

Unsure what to do next, she has almost made the decision to lie down and sleep when a slight breeze beckons from the back balcony that overlooks the top part of the town and the ridge. She lifts her weight from the bed and, kicking her flip-flops off en route, picks up the screwed-up list and puts it in the bin before she walks out onto the balcony and sits on the small metal chair.

She looks up to the ridge. Up there she was happy, looking for Yanni the donkey man. Then she had hope. Her shoulders droop and the corners of her mouth hang slackly. Marina sits slouched. The cement balcony is tiled. Most of the tiles are cracked. There are tiny sprouts of green life searching for sunlight in some of the cracks. One has a small yellow flower and a bee buzzes around it. It lands, and the stalk bends a little under its weight. It stays a moment before buzzing away. The stalk bounces back up, the tiny yellow head nodding. Marina sighs.

She pushes her weight forward and stands. She stuffs the flip-flops in her bag and puts on her old shoes. The hole in the toe might be beyond repair. Marina doesn't care. She would like to leave without having to see Zoe and her family. She does not want the jolly talk, the words of familiarity, the fond farewells. But there will be no avoiding it. Taking out her purse, she readies her money and is grateful she has the exact change. She makes sure all is left neatly and closes the door behind her.

She can hear the television but there are no other sounds. She knocks quietly. After a long pause Zoe answers, speaking in hushed tones as everyone is asleep, the heat being too much for them all. Marina feels guilty at the relief of not having to talk to anyone. Zoe expresses her joy at having Marina to stay and wishes her back soon. Marina asks her to pass on her good wishes to Bobby and Roula, and then she parts with a kiss on each of Zoe's cheeks. Zoe does not count the money, just stuffs it into her housecoat pocket and waves farewell with the parting words '*Sto kalo*' – go towards the good. Marina does not look back.

The taxi boats bob in the harbour. *Hera* is there and seems undamaged. Marina is pleased for Petta. She tries to cast away thoughts of Eleni. Why could she not find a good man like him?

An unfamiliar captain stands by his own taxi boat and Marina climbs on board without a word. The journey is silent except for the engine. She pays and leaves.

Her car is like an oven and the ballpoint pen on her dashboard has melted, dipping into an arch where one end was propped on a screwed-up petrol receipt. She opens all the doors but there is no breeze to cool the interior. Marina leans in and starts the engine, and waits in the shade of an olive tree for the air conditioning to take effect. Soon she grows impatient and climbs into the car, putting her bag on the passenger seat.

The steering wheel is almost too hot to touch. Many times she has considered buying a reflective silver windscreen visor, but she wonders if it would really have kept the car any cooler. The drive is insufferable. The roads pitted, winding and relentless. The landscape arid and monotonous.

The sight of the first house of her village gives her momentary joy but only because she knows she has a half bottle of ouzo at home. Anything to take off the edge of her emotions.

She pours the ouzo but doesn't drink. Her father drank ouzo when he was cross. Manolis drank it when he was cross, when he was happy, and when Mitsos, that rogue of a friend of his, was at the house. She takes the tiniest sip but it isn't what she wants. What she wants is to change things, and she knows this is not possible. So now she wants the next best thing: to change how she thinks about it. She crosses herself for strength. She rests her head back in the armchair.

The cockerels announce the new day, barking dogs accompanying. Shutters bang against whitewashed walls, as they are thrown open. The sun streams through the window and Marina looks about her to identify her surroundings. For a moment she is happy to be home but then the events of the previous day drag a faded black curtain across her future and she doesn't bother to stand. Eventually she has to go to the bathroom, and whilst she is there she makes the effort to have a shower. It revives her and she finds a little corner of reserve to take some action.

She dresses in her old black skirt and everyday black blouse. She takes out the box with her new shoes in from the wardrobe. They look very shiny. They fit well but feel stiff. The first walk they take with her is to the church.

The doors stand open. The smell of incense suffuses the still, chilled interior. There are several candles lit, standing in the sand in the prayer trays. Her neighbour is kissing the feet of a saint on one of the icons. She nods at Marina before crossing herself to leave.

Marina would like to talk to the papas. She wonders if he is around. She sits in one of the many wooden chairs that line the back and sides of the church. The two chandeliers are lit despite its being the middle of the day. There is brass and gold leaf in abundance. The panel at the front depicts Jesus and the archangels Michael and Gabriel. Each is embellished with ornate carved wooden surrounds painted gold, rising to the ceiling, fitted wall to wall. The gold reflects and dazzles. The candles' flickering flames are reflected in the golden surfaces. The lectern at the front is supported on brass eagles' wings. A brass pillar beside it supports a cascade of brass rings, each loaded with candles, descending in size one upon another, like tiers of a cake.

The ceiling is an intense pale blue dotted with golden stars. Gold and shimmering candles are everywhere.

Marina looks at the black-and-white tiled floor and tries to form her thoughts into what she should say to the papas. She is not sure how he will respond. Is it a sin against God? Will he condemn Eleni? Will he excommunicate her? Will he offer any comfort, any wisdom?

He appears from a side door. Marina is sure he is even fatter than the last time she saw him. His billowing black cassock dress stretches over his distended stomach. He could be having twins, his belly looks so tight. Marina giggles and the papas glances sternly in her direction. She bows her head and is thankful when he leaves.

She offers a prayer and crosses herself, and is about to go when she sees Juliet enter through the side door. Juliet must know the ways of the world. All Western woman are open and liberal, are they not?

Juliet caused such a stir when she first bought old Socrates' farm house. A stranger in the village. A British woman amongst them. She renovated that old place so beautifully and speaks such fluent Greek that now everyone forgets she has not been with them all her life. Just her blonde hair and her Western dress sense remind them. That and her silly accent. Marina giggles at the memory of some of her pronunciation, and Juliet notices her.

'*Geia sou*, Marina. How are you?'

'Hello, Juliet. I'm OK.' The tone of her voice betrays her. Juliet sits next to her and looks into her face. Marina is flustered under her scrutiny. 'Can I talk to you, Juliet?'

'Yes, of course.' Juliet settles herself.

'No, not here. I think what I have to say may be sinful,' Marina says. Juliet smirks but then tightens her lips; her eyes are shining and their corners crease. 'Come.' Marina stands and looks back at Juliet, beckoning her to follow.

Chapter 17

'That's when I saw this woman embrace her and kiss her like a man kisses a woman.' Marina reaches for a tissue from the table in the courtyard.

'And you object because…'

'People will talk. It may be a sin. I will have no son-in-law. No grandson.'

'But your other daughter will have many children, I am sure.'

'The doctor says maybe she cannot have children. For some time they are trying. And she has gone to Athens, and now she talks of America, besides she is not like me. But Eleni, she is very like me. If she had a son…'

Marina hesitates, but then turns to face Juliet and tells her about the son she had in the first year of marriage, who died. It feels safe talking to Juliet. She is an outsider, she is wise, she will not judge. Marina confides to her how she still mourns him. She decides to tell Juliet more, to relieve herself of some of her feelings to do with the island, when Juliet takes her hand.

'But,' Juliet says slowly, 'Eleni has her own life. Do you think she loves this woman?'

'It doesn't matter what she thinks she feels. I am sure it is a sin. Not to raise your own children! Besides, the village will gossip and chatter, and I will not be able to hold my head up.' A new wave of tears overcomes Marina. She rubs her scrunched-up paper hanky across her nose.

'So what you are saying is' – Juliet slows her speech and puts softness into the words – 'the gossip and chatter from your neighbours is more important than Eleni's happiness.'

Marina looks up at her sharply. 'No,' she snaps, and then looks down at her hands in her lap, which are pulling the tissue to pieces. 'Does it sound like that is what I am saying?'

'I am afraid that is the impression you have given me.' Juliet shifts her wooden chair nearer to Marina, their arms brushing, Juliet's hands on Marina's, the torn tissue buried. Marina can see the tiniest red vein in the inside corner of the white of one of Juliet's eyes.

'Marina, I know you were married to Manolis at your parents' bidding, but have you ever known love, the power of love, how it can lift you out of the ordinary and cause you to be able to do things beyond what you could imagine? It shapes you into a better person, it lifts your spirits where you can soar, it makes sense of life.'

Marina stops crying and looks across the courtyard, over the wall and into the blue sky. Juliet stays quiet.

'Once I knew love,' Marina begins. Juliet releases her hold and Marina puts the tissue on the table and takes a new one. 'So long ago.'

Marina drops her head and stares at the flagstones and along up to the plants by the wall. The wisteria needs watering again.

'We lived for a short while in the old town and my parents tried to get jobs. One night they told me we would be moving back to the village. I asked how this was possible as they had said, so many times, that our piece of land was not big enough for the three of us to survive on. But really I was wishing it was not true. I did not want to leave my friends. They said that they were joining farms with the neighbours and, when I asked how that was possible, that was when they told me I was pledged to be married to the neighbour – Manolis. I was without words, without understanding. I was fourteen at the time.'

Juliet reaches for a tissue.

'Well, I ran out of the house screaming that I would not do it. I ran through the old town until I came to the paved path that runs around by the sea. Here I began to walk. I was crying. I walked around to the point where the wind suddenly rushes at you and the lighthouse blinks on top of the metal tower.

'I sat on the concrete base of the lighthouse tower, watching the water swirling, letting the wind blow against me, blow away my tears. It was growing dark and the flashing light played with the waves. I had been sitting there for a few minutes when a voice said, "Are you OK?" and a boy shuffled from around the corner of the tower. He had also been sitting on the concrete plinth but out of sight. I was embarrassed because I had been crying and I was shy at first.'

Juliet quietly stands and takes a jug of water and glasses from just inside the kitchen and returns. Marina drinks deeply and wipes her mouth on her tissue.

'He was eighteen. He had just been served his papers to go into the army. They had stationed him all the way up in Thessaloniki. He was leaving the next day. He said he felt like his life was being stolen from him. I said I understood and I told him my story. He was angry on my behalf. He held me as I cried.'

Marina stands up and takes the jug of drinking water and pours what's left into the soil at the base of the wisteria.

'But we were kids and we were soon laughing over something, and we ran along the path by the sea to the beach and we played in the sand. We laughed so much. But slowly we grew tired and found a place between the rocks that was out of the sea breeze. We sat so close. Then he stroked my hair. His hand outlining my face, his fingertips electric on my skin. His face came closer, his eyes searching in mine, his breath on my mouth. Then he kissed me. My first kiss. I melted.

'He held me so close I thought I was disappearing into him. His words like jewels, each one reflecting

223

his beauty, our beauty. We talked and talked, our words turning to whispers. Before the morning we had pledged our love for each other. We talked of running away together, leaving the country. He had an uncle in Italy.

'We were woken by a dog sniffing at us. We called her Eros, god of love. The three of us walked slowly to the bus station. He had enough money to take us to Patra. From there we were going to work out how to get the money to take the boat to Italy. We were happy.

'It was at the bus station that his father found us. He cuffed him across the ears really hard and pulled him along the road by his shirt. When I tried to interfere he pushed me with such force that I fell backwards. A bus driver tried to protect me by holding me back. But as soon as he let go I ran after them.

'They had turned a corner and were gone. I spent all day roaming the old town for him. I didn't even know his name. I had called him Meli, because he was as sweet as honey. He called me Melissa, his little bee.'

Marina sits down again. Her body sags into her chair.

'Did you ever see him or hear from him again?'

'Never.'

Juliet sits silently with Marina and they watch a tomcat jump onto the wall and then climb down the wisteria stem. He pauses to wash himself before sniffing his way to the kitchen. Neither of them discourages him and so he steals inside. They hear the bin fall over and he comes running out with something in his mouth, streaks up over the wall, and is gone. A well-practised thief.

They can hear Costas talking to someone in the shop; the door from the courtyard is ajar.

Juliet speaks first.

'You see, the power of your love gave you the strength to make plans to leave the country without even enough money. I believe you would have succeeded, had his father not found you. If Eleni is in love she will have that power. She will overcome everything. She has everything she wants in her love.' Juliet takes a breath. 'Would you rather Eleni be happy or would you rather have a grandson by her?'

'That is not a question worth answering.' Marina gives Juliet a mock-chastising look before a new thought occurs to her. 'But what will her friends say when she comes home?'

Juliet laughs, but not harshly. 'They already know.'

'How can they already know? I have only just found out myself and I have told no one.'

'They will have known for years. I met Eleni once at Artemis's wedding and it was obvious to me.'

'What! You could tell? You can see it?'

'Me and everyone else who knows her.'

'Tell me this isn't so!' Marina stands but is unsure where to go and so makes a circuit round the courtyard. 'Her friends will know?' Juliet nods. 'The neighbours know?' Juliet nods again. 'Not the papas?' Juliet nods once more. 'Panayia!' Marina crosses herself. 'How can I believe this is true?'

Costas slips his head around the door to ask if they have any more boxes of crisps anywhere. Marina tells him they are in the storage room and he leaves to find them.

'There you are, an opportunity. I can hear people in the shop. Go ask them.'

'Oh yes, I will walk out there and say, "Hey did you know my daughter loves a woman?"'

'There is no need to be so blatant. Come, listen at the door. I will ask.'

'No! No, Tzuliet, I forbid you!' But Juliet has gone through the door. Marina hears pleasantries and then Juliet asks, 'Were you at school with Eleni?'

'Yes.' Marina can hear two voices but cannot place them. She looks through the crack in the door by the hinge but they are out of sight.

'Eleni has settled on the island, so I hear.'

'A nice place to be stationed,' one voice says.

'Yes, I think she will be happy there. Her lover lives on the island'

'Oh, she has found someone. That is good to hear. After her break-up with Katerina we thought her broken heart would never mend.' The other voice.

'Katerina?'

'Yes, you know, works in the hardware shop in town.' The first voice.

'Oh yes.'

'Here you go. How many bags do you want?' Costas's voice asks.

Juliet says her goodbyes, and there is a sound of coins dropping as she reappears in the courtyard.

'Katerina! Who works in the hardware shop? But her father is the prayer singer in the church,' Marina says, as Juliet sits down again. 'Who would have thought? Such a pretty girl. So delicate.'

'So, now you know that the rest of the world already knows, how do you feel about it?' Juliet asks.

'If there are no problems, then of course, I am happy for her. But what if she wants children? Do they want children?'

'They? Eleni is a "they" now?' Juliet laughs and opens the bag of crisps she brought back from the shop with her.

'You know what I mean.' Marina takes a crisp from the bag.

'They have only just got together. I think you are rushing things. But they are both capable of having children and there are ways, if that puts your mind at rest.'

Marina crunches. Her brow is furrowed and her eyes are not focused.

Juliet stays for something to eat and then sits for a while in the courtyard. The vines overhead protect them from the full strength of the sun. Marina pulls a weed or two from between the flags. Juliet dozes. The day slips away and Juliet announces that she must leave. They say a fonder goodbye than their hello, each giving the other's hand a squeeze as they kiss on both cheeks before parting.

Marina returns inside. She wanders upstairs to her daughters' bedroom. There are two little beds, Eleni's with a cloth rabbit sitting on the pillow. Marina picks it up and cuddles it.

The feeling starts somewhere in her stomach, quivering. It grows and fills her solar plexus and surges up her throat and escapes as a full belly laugh. Her angry, arguing, feisty Eleni has found her love and is happy. Marina pictures her smiling and at peace. Marina whoops with joy and throws the rabbit in the air. It hits the ceiling and comes back down. Marina fumbles the catch and picks it off the floor to return it to the bed, smoothing the sheets.

She wanders out of the girls' bedroom and into her own. Her bag sits on the chair. She opens it. The rapture she has just enjoyed mutates as she looks inside. The joy she feels for Eleni only serves to contrast with the deep despair she feels for herself. Tears begin to flow and she takes a handkerchief from the bag. The two embroidered butterflies dance with the movement as she takes it between both hands and presses it to her face. It smells of mothballs.

As she buries her face Marina weeps all the more. Her Eleni is happy, she is loved, and that is fantastic. Both her daughters are loved, their worlds are complete. There is no negative to focus on, no trouble to distract her, no matchmaking to take her attention. There is nothing to interfere with. Nothing to divert her. Her daughters' lives offer her no escape. In this new calm, her backdrop of misery cannot hide. The vein of bitterness and pain is highlighted in the peace. The person she must cry for now is herself. The person she must set free is Marina. She knows it is time. She must face the truth of what the island holds for her, find closure on her own life experiences.

She must return to the island again and find the people she needs to see.

Chapter 18

Marina is hoping Petta will be there to pick her up, but he isn't. She doesn't recognise the taxi boat man or his boat. The island appears to float on the water, looking harmless. She repeatedly tells herself that the pain she must face will lay her past to rest. It will be worth it.

A yacht passes them, its white sails billowing. One of the crew, clad in a black bikini, waves at her. Marina looks away. Her new shoes pinch a bit in the heat and she has spilt something on her black skirt. She scratches at it. The skirt seems baggy.

The boatman takes his money without a word. The pavement cafés are full of tourists fussing like chickens who have caught a mouse. Marina sees their smiling faces and turns away. She will take the path up through the town to Zoe's.

Yanni, waiting with his donkeys, nods at her. She nods back. His solemn face reflects her mood. She feels she understands him. She walks past to the lane that leads inland.

Up the steps and across the top. Past the shop that now extends for three windows and spills across the pavement. Marina pauses. Down the alley to her left, she remembers, there is a tiny church nestled in amongst the houses. She spontaneously takes the turning and pushes against the gnarled old studded arched door. It gives slowly and the air that rushes out smells of incense and wood polish and suspended time.

Inside it is still and cool. There are no electric lights and the narrow coloured windows provide very little illumination. There are three candles burning in a sand tray. The rich blue walls have been painted depicting saints and scenes from the Bible. Gold leaf provides shining halos and embellishments. There are nine chairs arranged in rows of three. They fill the space.

Marina sits on the front row and crosses herself.

'OK, Marina, old girl, let's get all the help we can,' she says to herself before bending her head and reciting prayers by rote, bringing back memories of her childhood. Completing the ritual, she talks directly to the painting of the saint on the templon that hides the altar.

'So Panayia, mother of God,' she concludes, 'I need some strength and some wisdom and a little bit of Greek serendipity. Please.' She stands and lights a candle and places it centrally in the nearest sand tray at the front.

'Excuse me,' a thin voice enquires. 'How are you, my dear?'

Marina turns to see a diminutive lady, not more than four and half feet tall. She is wearing black from head to foot and has on a scarf tied to cover her head and chin in traditional peasant fashion. She has the kindest eyes and there is something familiar about her smile, but Marina cannot place her.

'I am well, and you?' She searches the old woman's face.

'You don't remember me?' The old lady sits on one of the wooden chairs at the front. Marina helps her as she wobbles. 'I remember you, such a sad, sweet time.'

'I am sorry, I think you must have mistaken me for someone else.'

'Have you ever embroidered a hanky with black butterflies?'

Marina frowns before her eyes widen. She takes hold of the back of the chair next to the woman to regain some stability before she eases her weight down onto the rush seat. No one knows about her embroidering the black butterflies. Except Aunt Efi, and she is dead. Marina crosses herself.

'It was such a sad, sweet time. You were so young.'

'Please, who are you?' Marina asks.

'Let it come slowly, my dear.' The lady pats Marina's hand.

Marina searches for who this woman can be but is at a loss. She raises her hands palms upwards and shrugs.

'How long were you here on the island for? It did seem a long time, and all that time you were shut up in that apartment with no one to play with, not even your mother by your side.'

'My dad wouldn't let my mum come. He said he needed her at home.' Marina's lower lip begins to tremble as the years fall away. The old lady strokes her arm, comforting, caring. 'I spent all day, every day in that apartment. That's when I started embroidering everything in sight with the black butterflies that would land on the window sills and tease me with their freedom. I wasn't allowed to go out to play, to see anyone, just Aunt Efi.'

'You didn't go out at all?'

A momentary smile plays around the corners of Marina's mouth. 'I did sneak out a couple of times when she was asleep.'

'Where did you go?'

'Once I went up on the top road that joins the coastal path to the boatyard, and once I found a door open that had no handle. The smell of honey and wax was amazing and there was an old…' Marina's jaw drops open. 'No! It cannot be! That would make you…'

'Ninety. It's not so old these days.' There is a ringing sound, abrasive within the hushed stone walls. Marina looks about the church for the cause and the old lady takes a mobile phone out of her pocket.

'No, I am fine, dear. I am in the church with an old friend. Yes, goodbye.' She puts the phone away. 'My daughter, always checking on me, not a moment's peace.'

'So you are the candle-making lady.' Marina reaches out to take her hands. The lady nods and smiles.

Marina's smile is suddenly gone and she lets go of the old lady's hands.

Marina recalls something unpleasant. The old lady nods again. 'That was me too. Yanni the donkey man's *yiayia* was on the ridge. She could not come down in time. She was dealing with her own daughter. I saw your Aunt Efi running in panic, so I came. It was not so bad though, was it, my dear? You were very quick. Not even an hour or so, if I remember correctly.'

Marina is silently crying. She searches in her pockets and brings out a handkerchief, with black butterflies embroidered on it. Marina's silent tears become audible at the sight of it.

'It was a beautiful and sad time,' the lady says.

'I had just turned fourteen. The year before they married me off.' Marina feels the waves of emotion will drown her. She struggles for breath. The lump in her throat will not be swallowed. Her head spins, her temples throb.

The lady quietly stands and takes Marina's butterfly hanky, and dips it in the font and wrings it out. She returns and places it in Marina's hand and guides it to her forehead.

Marina's eyes will not focus. The muscles under her lower lip twitch and she cannot stop the corners of her mouth being dragged down. Images of the candle lady's kindness mix with the pain. Aunt Efi speaking in harsh tones. Urgency. The spasms that took away Marina's control. The fear of tearing in two. The donkeys braying outside the window, competing with her own cries. The cold cloth on her forehead. The narrow bed that she slid from, onto the floor. Aunt Efi mopping up the wet. The spasms coming faster, more urgently. The overwhelming fear. The candle lady calling her name, telling her, 'All will be well, soon it will be over. Breathe, my sweet, breathe.' Aunt Efi shouting, 'Maria, hold her still.'

It went on and on. The panting. Aunt Efi praying. Maria stroking her hair, her face close, comforting. Another wave. Being transported by the spasms out of reality. The intensity of the focus. Her energy draining away. The ability to cope slipping from her. Becoming lost. Everything slack. And then, suddenly, the pain had all gone. A wave of exhaustion, the elation of still being alive. The uncertainty of what had just happened.

Maria, the candle lady, lifted the blood-covered crying bundle onto her chest and she fell in love with one look in his eyes. He had hair, blonde, like Meli's, and he had Meli's eyes. All the love she needed for herself flowed from her to him, all the love she had held precious for Meli himself flowed to this tiny Meli. Just as she had sunk with the pain, she soared with the love. She floated above Aunt Efi. The world disappeared.

'It was – he was – the most beautiful thing I had ever seen.'

'He was, my dear. He was perfect.'

'They took him.'

'I know.' The lady wipes her own tears.

'One month they gave me to suckle him, and then they took him.' Marina can hold the emotions back no longer. Her body shakes, the repressed memories flood back, the pain, the loss, the powerlessness. Losing him felt like part of her soul was ripped from her. Marina feels the breaking down, the releasing of years of denied love and grief and loss. Her love flows afresh, huge, threatening to burst through her chest. It rises to her throat but there is no escape. It comes in bursts of sobs and tears

'You were so young, so young.' The lady nods and she sits and holds Marina, watching her candle burn away. The stillness of the church holding them both. Timeless.

The candle has burnt away by the time Marina's sobbing stops. Maria is still holding her. She moves to free herself and Maria lets go.

Marina sits for a moment to gather herself.

'I was here from the week after they found out I was pregnant until the month after his birth. They hid me here so they would not lose the chance of marrying me to Manolis.'

'I remember. Your aunt told me.'

'I had another son by Manolis just a year later. But it pained me to see him. My heart would break for my firstborn. So my mother tried to raise him. He was sickly from the first.'

'It happens. Did he die?'

'Yes, but I could not mourn his loss without mourning the loss of my first love, and that was forbidden, so I did not mourn at all. I just blamed myself.'

'Your life has been harsh enough without you adding to it with self-blame, my dear.'

Marina laughs dryly. There is a pause. The church waits.

'So why are you here now?' The question hangs in the incense-filled air.

'My daughter told me she has a lover from here.' Marina feels the enormity of what could have been.

'Ah, so you need to know if it is your son. Yes, that would be very difficult. I take it she does not know of your firstborn?'

'But I have found out it is not him. It is someone else.'

'And your son? I think perhaps you have not found him yet. Your crying days would be over, I think, if you found him.'

'There are so few of the right age that still live here. I have ruled some of them out, but mostly I was ruling them out as my daughter's lover rather than considering the possibility of them being my son.'

'Yes, I can see why that would take precedence. And now?'

'And now I need to know. If he knows, he will probably hate me for abandoning him. If he doesn't know, I don't know what I will do.' Marina lights another candle. 'I don't even know how to find him.'

'I do.'

Chapter 19

Marina feels her legs give. She flushes hotly and fans herself with her hand. 'I need some air.'

Marina and Maria leave arm in arm and sit on the stone plinth outside the church door. A donkey is tied up nearby and it shifts its weight, hooves scraping against the flags. The wood and leather saddle creaks. The passage feels hot despite the whitewashed walls casting shade.

'Does he know?' Marina asks.

'There was never a time he didn't know.'

Marina can feel her heart racing. 'Does he hate me?'

'How could he hate you? He doesn't know you,' Maria says slowly with a smile.

'Would he want to meet me?' Her mouth has gone dry. She stands, with the intention of going to the three-windowed shop and getting some water. Maria stands beside her. Her phone rings and she fumbles to answer it.

'Yes, all right, dear. Bye.' She pockets the phone. 'It seems I am wanted at home.' She starts to walk towards the main path where the shop displays its goods.

'Do you…' Marina can hardly force herself to ask the question. It could be Costas, the millionaire waiter. It could be Socrates, the nervous papas. It is not Panos. He said he looks like his mum. It is not Yanni the donkey man, since his *yiayia* was helping with his birth the same day Marina had her son, which is why she did not attend as midwife and Maria was called upon.

God forbid it could be Aris Kranidiotis, the jewellery man, although it is possible. It is also possible that it is the boatyard man, but Marina has the impression he is like his brother so it seems unlikely. And then there is Alexandros Mavromatis, whom she did not manage to track down before finding out the truth about Eleni's lover.

The thought of Eleni distracts her. They still haven't talked to resolve their issues. Marina feels differently about her now, more relaxed. But for Eleni's sake she must heal the rift.

'Do I what?' Maria asks, bringing Marina out of her thoughts.

'Oh! Yes. Do you…' Marina swallows again. 'Do you know who he is, or where he lives?'

'Oh yes. Alexandros. Aleko for short. He lives there, on the corner.' Maria points down the steps towards Zoe's house. There are three doorways at that wide crossroads. Marina's head is swimming from the knowledge of his name. She rolls the full name on her tongue as if she has never said it before – Alexandros – and then clicks out several 'Alekos' and giggles. Her broad smile betrays her delight, but her eyes reflect her nervousness. Maria's phone rings again and she takes her time to answer. She is curt and pops the phone back in her skirt pocket.

'I must go, Marina. It has been such a pleasure to see you again. Do let me know how things turn out.' At this moment, a middle-aged woman bustles around the corner in a housecoat.

'Mother, come on. We are waiting for you.' The housecoated woman addresses Maria. She nods politely at Marina as she takes her mother by the arm, talking away at her about wandering off and staying out too long.

Marina looks down to the crossroads. Her eyes water, her cheeks flush. She frowns, smiles, and frowns again.

'What's the worst that could happen, Marina, old girl?' she asks herself. 'Well, he could reject me, he could shout at me for abandoning him all those years ago, he could ignore me.' She shivers. Her mouth is dry. She goes into the shop to buy a small bottle of water and then realises that she has left her bag in the church. She hurries back to collect it, and lights another candle, briefly asking all the gods and saints for strength and a good outcome.

She walks slowly to the top of the steps by the apartment where he was born all those thirty-five years ago. The sight of the door to the apartment holds no emotion for her now. She has greater things to deal with, bigger fears. She looks down to the crossed paths at the square at the bottom of the steps. A massive eucalyptus shades half the area. There's a bench, and cats are lazing, cooling themselves on the stone flags. The whitewash on the left-hand wall has become grey with time. It looks dark in the shadow of the tree.

Marina considers that she has to go down there anyway to check into Zoe's on the opposite corner. On the near left-hand corner is Irini's house, so Alexandros's, Alekos's, house must be the one on the right with the greying wall and the bench outside. The door in the wall looks shabby, its paint peeling. A bougainvillea is growing over the wall from the inside. Purple flowers add colour to the sun-whitened scene. The house behind the wall is hidden by the branches of the eucalyptus. Marina begins her descent.

Despite the aid of gravity, it feels harder to go down the steep steps now than it felt to go up them the time she fell and hit her head. That seems like a lifetime ago, and yet how long was it? A couple of weeks? Backwards and forwards across the water, mainland to island, up and down in her car, coast to coast, the stress of Eleni all mixed in. Marina has lost track of what day it is. The peeling door looks so tightly shut.

Each step down brings tears. Each step brings a nervous smile of hope. Her knees are weak. Her new shoes are dusty and they are not as comfortable as her old shoes. Will she recognise him? Will Zoe have room still? Will he be tall? Is Costas managing the shop all right? Will Eleni ever forgive her for keeping her brother a secret? Will Artemis? Will he call her

Mum or Marina? She runs out of distracting questions as she draws near to the bottom of the steps.

Three, two, one, she is there. The crossing of paths, the square on the edge of the short path to Zoe's, the open area at the bottom of the steps where her son lives.

Marina's hands are trembling and her legs are like jelly. Her big bag feels too heavy all of a sudden. She sits on the bench by the tightly closed grey peeling door.

She cannot do it. She cannot knock on this stranger's door and say, 'Hello, I am your mum.' Abandoning him was wrong. How could he forgive her? How will he understand she had no choice? How could he hear the screams she made when they took him, all those years ago? He could never know the hopelessness she felt in losing him, the chasm in her life. The blame she heaped on herself over the years. The love she felt for his father. The passion she has for him, even though she has never known him.

She must book in at Zoe's. There is no rush to knock on the door. She has waited thirty-five years. An hour, a day, a week longer will not make any difference now.

A movement catches her attention. There is someone walking towards her, coming up from the harbour. For a moment she envisages it could be him, her long-lost son. But as he moves out of direct glaring sunlight into the shadows she recognises the size and demeanour of the dancing captain.

Marina dries her eyes and puts her hanky away in her bag. As he draws near, he waves.

'Well, hello, my friend.' He is grinning.

'Well, hello, right back at you. How are you? Did they patch you up all right?'

'Ah! A bruise and a bandage and I am as good as new.' He sits on the bench next to her.

'The boat looks unharmed.'

He snorts. 'Yes, unharmed and untouchable.'

'How so?'

'My friend who lent me the boat, the job for the summer, has asked me kindly not to use it again. He cannot afford to lose it. He is now thinking of coming home, so I may have no home as well.'

'Oh, that is very bad news. But the boat was unharmed. Was the incident your fault?'

'Well, this is what I say to him. The engine, she cuts. The anchor will not bite. So I tie her to a rock. The weather is good, a little windy perhaps. Then I roll up my sleeves and I take a look at the engine.' He rubs his bruised arm and lifts his shirt off his bandaged shoulder.

'I cannot find the problem with the engine. I try and try until the battery she goes flat. The VHF radio runs on battery. So what to do? The wind has picked up and I feel the boat and me are no longer safe. So I call Irini on my mobile but the signal is weak. So I try the port police and they hear enough to come for me.'

'Well, that all sounds very sensible. So what is your friend's problem?'

'I should have gone around Ship Rock, not between it and the shore. So I say to my friend I will go around next time, but now he is worried. He will not let go of the idea that I will wreck his boat. But it is his boat, and it is his living, so I understand his thinking. I am grateful for the time I have had. It is just tough on Irini.' His voice is low and quiet.

'On both of you. What will you do?'

'Who knows?' he says briskly, as if he hasn't a care in the world. 'Let's talk about you. How are you, my friend?'

'*Etsi-ketsi*, as they say. So-so.'

'Only so-so? A wonderful woman like you should be having a marvellous time, always.'

Marina smiles but she cannot hide her nervousness, which makes her tremble and her eyes fill with tears.

'Oh my, you have tears in your eyes. My lovely friend, tell me what concerns you?'

Marina feels she needs a friend. Besides, he may know Alexandros. He might know the best way for her to let him know she is here.

'It is difficult, sometimes.'

'Life is difficult all the time. If it was not we would forget we were alive. Like when we are happy, we only realise afterwards that we were happy. We miss it when it is happening. So if we were happy all the time we would miss our lives.' He speaks with a light tone, his mouth twisting into a smile, trying to cheer her up.

'What nonsense.' Marina is smiling.

'Maybe, maybe not.'

'Well, this bit of my life could be happy or unhappy, depending on the result.'

'Ah, well, there is your problem.' He smiles again.

'Where is my problem?'

'In wanting a particular result. If you just wanted the event and the result didn't matter, then happy or unhappy would not come into it.'

'Now I know you are talking nonsense.' Marina decides to play him at his own game. 'Everything we do is in the pursuit of happiness. You rang the port police because being rescued would bring you greater happiness than you dying. You were there on the water in the first place to earn a wage, which buys you food for your stomach, which makes you happier than being hungry. We all do exactly what we want to do at any given time in the pursuit of our individual happiness. Unless we are forced by others to do otherwise.'

'So there you go!'

'Where do I go?'

'You have answered your own problem. It sounds like, regardless of whether the outcome is happy or sad, whatever this event is that is in your life will happen anyway. If it is happening because you want it to happen, you are doing what you want to do in pursuit of your own happiness. So by making it happen you will be happy whether the outcome is happy or unhappy.'

'Utter and absolute nonsense.' But Marina is not sure if she follows him or not. Maybe he has made a valid point and she has missed it.

'So come, tell me, what is the problem, and no riddles?' He is no longer smiling.

'OK.' Marina feels lifted by his chatter. She feels the problem is not insurmountable now. She feels supported. She will face it. 'Many years ago I lost track of someone very dear to me. I did not want to lose him, it pained me very much, but I was young and many decisions were made for me. The loss of this person has caused me much pain and sadness in my life. Now I have found out where he is so I wish to take the goat by the horns and meet him, face to face. If I am rejected, then so be it, but I am hoping that is not how it will be.'

'Ah, a matter of the heart. Hearts are tricky things. Sometimes when we get what we think we want, that too can be painful.'

'At last you speak a true word.' There is a slight breeze and the eucalyptus leaves rustle and one or two lightly shower upon them, spinning silver and blue-green as they fall. 'I am sitting here trying to decide the best way to approach this person. Whether to just knock on his door and say, "Hello, it's me," or whether that would be too much of a shock. Maybe it would be better to get someone to tell him I am here and arrange a meeting, and then he can come if he wants to, or not if he doesn't.'

'Hmm. That would be a very kind and thoughtful way to meet him. But if he does not come you have deprived yourself of the sight of him, and he has been deprived of the sight of you, which may alter his nerve. It might give him courage, perhaps, if he sees you.'

'But to just knock on his door and say who I am?'

'Will he not recognise you?'

'I cannot think how to bring the subject up gently.'

Marina falls silent and they sit side by side. The sun is beginning to set and there is a pink glow to the hills, the houses and the whitewashed walls. The cats stretch in the cooling air. Someone plays the bouzouki, a slow haunting melody.

Marina wonders if she should knock on the door at all. Her visit to the island has brought her friends. Her life is richer for having visited. Maybe she should be content with that. But the same old gnawing hollowness opens in her chest at the thought of walking away, and silent tears begin their well-worn course down her cheeks. The same feeling as a hundred times before.

Her chin jerks back and she blinks hard. This is the feeling that keeps her distant from Eleni and Artemis. This is the feeling she does anything to avoid. If she allowed herself to love Eleni and Artemis with all her heart, as she loved her son, and she lost them too, this would be the pain that remained. Marina is appalled that at some point in her life she has made the decision not to love her children fully for fear of the pain that losing them might bring.

Marina's life falls into clear focus. In her fear of losing them she has driven them away. The love they needed was not to be found at home. Artemis went to America chasing love and is now on her second marriage. Eleni, more sensitive than Artemis, hardened her heart and left for Piraeus at the earliest opportunity to join the port police. In her own words, 'To be part of something, to belong.' Both chose paths that took them away from her and towards a place where they were needed, a place of belonging. Marina sits, stunned by her revelation. Her self-protective actions have brought her nothing but loneliness and misery. But, worse than that, far worse than that, she has been a bad mother.

With no warning – Petta in the middle of stretching his legs forward and leaning back, his hands interlocked behind his head, Marina still sitting upright – she melts into series of deep soul-wrenching sobs. Petta sits up and smiles, as if mistaking her movement and noise for chuckles. But in an instant his smile is lost and his face is all consternation. He releases his interlocked hands and wraps them around Marina.

'Oh my, oh my. My dear friend. Believe me, it will never be as bad as you imagine.' Keeping one arm around her shoulders he begins to search for his hanky to offer her. Marina leans forward to take hers from her bag. They find them simultaneously.

The breeze stops. The leaves hang suspended. Marina ceases sobbing and stares. Petta abruptly quiets his cooing talk and blinks several times.

In their grasp, between the two of them, are four black butterflies. Two on each hanky. Marina's lips drop apart. She looks in his eyes to recognise him. He scans her face, his mouth opening and closing as if to form words that will not come. He then begins a smile.

'This person you have not seen...' His words are coming out shaky and cracked.

Marina can feel a smile building. 'Yes?' It does not sound like her own voice.

'You would not, by chance, have last seen him thirty-five years ago?'

Marina can force no noise from her throat, so she just nods.

'Would he have been very, very young when you left him?' His voice has broken into a quiet high pitch, suppressing tears.

Marina nods again.

His bottom lip is all aquiver and his tears now spill over the rims of his eyes. His age drops away as he becomes a boy again, and without another word he lowers his head and leans into Marina's chest. She wraps both arms around his head and tentatively kisses his hair. He smells lovely, of shampoo and sea. She kisses his hair again and leans her cheek against the top of his head. She feels complete. They remain still, lost in time, making up the years until the sun sets.

Petta makes the first move to be released. He straightens and rubs his back. They have been still a long time. As if they are in agreement, no words are spoken. Marina reaches down for her bag. She pulls it onto her knee and begins to take out gaily wrapped parcels. The pile of parcels grows. Petta picks one up. He holds it closer to read the inscription.

For my beloved son on his twenty-first birthday.

He picks up another.

For my beloved son on his thirteenth birthday.

He looks at the growing pile on the bench between them and begins to count.

'There are thirty-five,' Marina says.

Chapter 20

Petta opens one for himself, aged two. It is a blue hand towel with two butterflies embroidered on it.

'You know, everyone thinks my nickname "Petalouda" – butterfly – is because I fluttered from girl to girl.' Petta shakes his head, 'But Mum and Dad called me it first because you had insisted that I have the hankies you embroidered for me.' He pauses. 'Mum said you would come to find me one day.'

Marina takes in the reality that someone else is Petta's mum. 'Who is she?'

'Vasso Mavromati. They have the small farm on the way to the coastal path.'

'With the white horse under the tree?'

Petta laughs. 'Yes, but not all the time.'

'Hello! What are you guys cooking up?'

'Irini!' Petta jumps from his seat. 'Guess who I have found.'

'Er, Marina?' Irini smiles and scans the pile of little parcels. She moves closer and picks one up. She reads the inscription.

'You have to be kidding?' Irini's eyes are wide, she starts to take small jumps on the spot.

'Irini,' Petta announces in a serious voice. 'Meet my mother.'

Irini looks from him to her. Her hand reaches out to touch Petta whilst the rest of her moves in to hug Marina.

'This is fantastic news! Petta, I am so happy for you.'

The three of them ask questions back and forth. Marina encourages him to have thirty-five birthdays all at once. But Petta says he wants to save them. Take it slowly. They chatter on, but it is getting very dark so Irini suggests they move to the house, where she has cooked, so there is food if they are hungry. They sit on the terrace outside. The food is almost forgotten but the chilled wine cools them. The warm night air takes the heat off the day. The crickets still sing but the cicadas have stopped now the temperature has dropped. The island is dark. The sky is clear and the stars seem near enough to reach up and touch them.

The night becomes early morning and they are still talking. Details of each other's lives, events that shaped them. Marina holds nothing back. Her love for him flows wide and sure and strong. She is healing with each breath she takes and every word he speaks to her.

'So, I have two sisters?' Petta's eyes are so bright.

'Artemis is married and in Athens, and Eleni is here on the island.'

'Here! On this island?' He jumps off his seat. 'We must go see her!'

'Sit down, you big butterfly! It is two thirty in the morning. Now is not the best time to make a good impression.' Irini laughs.

'Two thirty. Oh dear, Zoe will be in bed.' Marina picks up her empty bag.

'Marina, lady, Mum, Mother, you need no Zoe. We have a spare room.' Petta laughs at his own indecision as to how to address her. Irini goes inside the house.

'Perhaps "Marina" is best.' Marina blushes.

'OK, Mum,' Petta replies. Marina giggles.

Irini returns. 'Clean sheets on the bed, Mum-in-law-to-be.'

'Thank you, Irini, and I think I had better go and lie on it or I will never get up in the morning.' She stands with her empty bag and Petta also stands to give her another hug and a kiss goodnight. Irini shows her to her room.

Marina is the first up. She makes herself a Greek coffee on the camping gas stove by the sink. For years she has made her coffee on a portable camping gas stove, as have all her friends and many of the *kafeneio* owners, who make hundreds a day. In fact, all of Greece makes Greek coffee this way. Today, her lucid mind wonders why. Why use the small stove when there is a cooker? But the question only holds her interest for a second or two. She looks out of the window over to Zoe's house as she waits for the coffee to boil. The sun is bright and the heat has already begun. A donkey brays and she can hear goat bells up in the hills. A woman in black walks into the square and sits on the bench that Marina sat on the night before. The woman has a silver foil parcel, and the collection of cats that are gathering around her feet offers a clue about the contents.

The woman puts the opened foil on the ground and there are hisses and paw pats until they have a piece each and they all stand hunched, protecting their breakfasts. Once they have eaten they return to the foil, but it is empty and licked clean. The lady in black wraps up the foil and stands. The cats prowl around her like sharks. She wanders back down the path.

'Panayia! Oh dear.' Marina's coffee boils over and she whips the pan from the stove. There are coffee grounds all over the stove and the sink. But – and Marina is thankful for this – there is enough coffee left in the pan to fill a cup. She cleans the mess and takes her coffee out onto the terrace.

There are birds singing and in the corner of the garden is a lilac bush with butterflies all over it. Black ones, and red admirals. The borders need weeding, though, and some flowers need planting. A few annuals would add colour. She makes a mental note to buy some for Petta and Irini but remembers that the houseowner is coming back. This thought makes way for the next. If Petta and Irini are without a job with a future, why not have them take over the shop? Marina could retire. Cook the meals, tend the plants, organise the workers for her orange orchards a bit better. It could work out very nicely. With such security, Petta and Irini could get married.

'*Kalimera, Mitera.*' Petta tries a formal greeting. Marina is on her feet and the two hug again.

'I'll make you a coffee,' she offers.

'Irini's beaten you to it.' Irini comes out, two cups in hand.

The chatter begins again – clarification of what was said the night before, new snippets they have remembered of their lives that they want to tell. Petta moves the conversation to the future and what that brings them all. At this point Marina offers them the shop and her home to share. They are overwhelmed. Petta asks if she understands what it is that she is offering – security, a future, a home. Marina dismisses it as being useful for her so she can concentrate on arranging the workers in the orange groves better. It will give her time to weed and water the garden, to cook dinner. Petta is lost for words until he says to Irini that they can now get married. Irini begins to cry. He brings out the ouzo to celebrate but it sits untouched as they drink their coffee. The conversation never stops, and Petta remembers about his new-found siblings.

'So, my sisters! Eleni is here, you say?'

Marina then has the grim duty of telling Petta of the rift that has grown between her and Eleni. But she does not mention yesterday's revelation of her fear of loving her children. Today, she can love them with all her heart.

'Then we must fill this rift! We must see her and become a family. I have waited thirty-five years with no brothers or sisters, so there will be no rift big enough to divide us now!'

Petta's positive attitude smothers Marina's misgivings. She may feel very different towards Eleni now, but there is no reason for Eleni to feel differently towards her. She wonders if her confession of her secret son will help or hinder.

'Why so glum?' Petta asks.

'You don't know Eleni. She is like fire, she burns. She shouts and bangs doors and walks away. There is no talking to her.' Petta offers his own embroidered handkerchief, which makes Marina smile.

'How many did I leave you with?'

'I don't know. I have three left. I wash them by hand so they will last.' Marina is touched and her tears come from gratitude. 'Perhaps you need to make me some more?'

Marina chuckles.

'So, come on, where will we find Eleni?' Petta stands.

Marina is not ready to face her. She needs to prepare, practise phrasing, making it softer, easier for Eleni to handle. She is not ready. When Petta offers his hand to help her stand she cannot refuse him, but voices her concerns about it being too soon. Petta asks again where Eleni will be.

'She may be at work or – I don't know, really. Her girlfriend is friends with Panos, who has the barber's shop.

'No! Panos – Pan. Then she keeps good company. He was my classmate and a finer man you could not find in all of Greece. Come, let us go see Pan.'

'But, I…'

'Leave it to me,' Petta says as they all mount the stairs up to Panos's barbershop. 'Hey, Pan,' he calls as he gets to the top of the stairs, and the room opens out, the patchwork floor-to-ceiling, wall-to-wall windows just as stunning as Marina remembers, overlooking the harbour.

The town looks unreal, like a board game. Marina would like an island version of Monopoly, a game she has played on occasion since they brought out the Greek version. She giggles at the thought. The playing pieces will be a donkey, a water taxi, a handcart. She looks through the windows for more ideas but she finds it difficult to focus as her eyes swim with tears.

'Hey Petta, how are you running?' Panos asks in young people's talk.

Marina chuckles again; you can't ask old people that, as they cannot run. The chuckle lingers and she realises how nervous she feels.

'Hello, lady whose son wants to work as a hairdresser on another island…'

Marina feels her cheeks warming. His tone tells her that he never believed her tale. Marina looks around the room and is relieved no one else is there.

Petta laughs – last night Marina told him the story of her first visit to Panos – before proudly telling Panos who Marina is to him. Panos congratulates her. She thanks him in a formal way, a little embarrassed at having lied to him. But Petta is speaking over the top of them, telling Panos who his sister is. Marina is stunned by his openness, his lack of discretion. She wants him to stop, to think about Eleni, about her. He doesn't realise what he is doing. Her instinct tells her to leave, but at that moment a happy Irini puts an arm through hers. She is smiling from ear to ear.

Panos says he will call Eleni immediately and picks up his phone.

'Stop, everyone, stop.' Marina puts her hands up to halt everything. 'Eleni is angry with me. This is not the way to deal with it. First I need to address that before we shock her with this news.'

'Eleni is not angry with you!' Panos sounds surprised. 'Eleni is terrified she cannot please you. She has made you sound like some ogre. Although having met you twice I cannot see why.' He smiles at her. But Marina does not respond; she is thinking of facing Eleni.

'She wants to please me! My God, she is the one without a flaw! She is perfect! She is funny and bright and confident and independent and all the things I never was. I adore her and all she has to do is breathe and she pleases me. It is I who am trying to please her.'

'Huh, I wish!'

Marina spins round to see Eleni in the doorway with Anna.

'Eleni!'

'Why are you here? To interfere?'

'No, I have come to try to make things right with you.' Marina can hear her tone of voice and wishes it didn't sound so harsh.

'Mum, we need to talk. But not here, not now. I need to say some things you are not going to like.'

'Pano, can they borrow your room for a little?' Petta asks. Panos is already heading for the door. He shows all the signs of being uncomfortable with the situation and cannot wait to leave. He pulls Petta with him and Irini follows. Marina pleads with her eyes for them to stay. Eleni can shout as loud as Manolis used to. Calming Anna hesitates to leave, but Irini pulls on her sleeve and then Marina and Eleni are alone. They turn in unison to look down over the harbour. They say nothing. They watch lithe Panos, stocky Petta, tiny Irini and graceful Anna walk across the harbour and sit down outside one of the cafés.

'Eleni…' But Marina does not know what she is going to say, and pauses.

'No, Mum, I need to say something first and then you can decide if you want to say whatever it is you have come here to say.'

'OK, but I think I know.'

'You know nothing about me.' She is shouting already and Marina backs away a little. Eleni steps behind the barber's chair, a physical barrier between them. 'I have felt very lonely for a long time. I don't think you know how lonely.' She drops her head and Marina steps forward to comfort her, but Eleni brings her head up sharply and Marina stops moving. 'When Dad died I felt lost.' Marina's eyes widen. 'Don't worry, I know he was no good, but whilst he was alive he was my excuse for why things felt bad.' Eleni sighs and steps part way around the chair. 'When he was gone I had no more excuses. I found someone to give me comfort in the village but it wasn't complete. I still felt lonely. I felt I could not please you. That's when I ran away to Piraeus.' Marina opens her mouth to speak but Eleni holds up a warning finger.

'I found rules and regulations which I understood and they made my life safe, but still something was missing.' She looks at Marina to see if she understands. Marina is silent, and Eleni steps from behind the chair into open ground. 'I came on a training weekend here, and that is when I found the missing piece. I told you I had found someone who made me feel complete, loved.' Marina smiles to show her approval. 'But you talked of weddings and grandchildren and I felt I had let you down.' Marina shakes her head, but Eleni is looking at the floor. 'I know Artemis cannot give you the grandchildren you desire.' She lifts her head, stands with her feet shoulder width apart, arms by her side as though she is on parade. 'And I don't want to – that is not how my life is going to be.' There is defiance in her voice. Marina opens her mouth again but Eleni hisses a sharp 'Shh'.

'Then Petta was nearly killed and I was nearly drowned. I saw how quickly life can be taken from you. That is when I made the decision that you must be told.' Marina takes a step towards her. 'I cannot go on living my life in half-truth trying to please you, Mum. You will hear the truth and then you can decide how you want to behave and whether you still want to talk to me.'

'Eleni–'

'Hush. Mum, you need to know that–'

'–that Anna is your girlfriend?'

'You know!'

'Yes, I know, and I liked her from the first time I saw her.'

'The first time you saw her?'

'Yes. But Eleni, it is not I who has to decide if I will talk to you. It is you who must decide if you will talk to me.'

'What?'

Marina cannot look at Eleni as she says, 'I have held a secret from you all your life.' She can feel Eleni's eyes on her. 'This secret…' Marina bites her bottom lip to hold back her emotions; she must say what she must say, with no interruptions. 'This secret has made me a bad mother…'

'Oh no!' Eleni takes a step towards her.

'Yes, I know it has. It has stopped me loving you as you deserve. I am sorry, so, so sorry, and for this I can never forgive myself, and I can only hope you can understand and forgive me to a degree, although I do not deserve it.' Marina takes out her handkerchief.

'Mum, what are you saying? It is I who rejected you, because of Dad, because I couldn't please you and because I thought you would push me away if you knew about Anna.'

'No, Eleni, it is I who rejected you and I have kept something very important from you.'

The door opens suddenly.

'Have you told her yet?' Petta's head is visible around the door.

'Told me what?' Eleni asks.

'Your poor mum, they were very mean to her when she found love. She had me and they took me away. I am your brother, Eleni!'

'What the…' Eleni backs away from Petta, who is advancing with open arms. Marina is frozen in astonishment.

Anna appears at the door. 'Eleni, are you ok? Petta just told me.'

'I…' Eleni looks to her mother and then her new-found brother. 'So all this time that I had my secrets from you, you had even bigger ones from me?' Marina cannot read Eleni's emotions and backs away to stay safe.

'Like mother, like daughter,' Petta laughs, but neither Eleni nor her mother smiles. They each wait for the other's reaction. The room becomes still. Panos enters quietly. The room is crackling in its silence.

Chapter 21

It is a stand-off. Two and two stand opposite each other. Marina, dressed in faded black, is by the window. Petta is at her side, a pleading look on his face, gazing across at Eleni. Eleni, in her port police uniform, stands rigid. Calm, elegant Anna is by her side, squeezing her hand. Panos stands motionless by the door, contemplating the group, each person waiting to see what the others will do.

Anna notices the dust floating between them, like tiny sparks in the sun's rays. Swirls and calms, each speck hovering, alive, until it is suddenly snuffed out by a shift in the air.

'May I say something?' she asks quietly in the stillness. No one replies. 'We are all alive. No one has died.' Everyone, including Panos, who was edging back out of the door, looks at her quizzically. 'I know Irini, because Irini and I have something in common. Both our parents are dead. They were too young to die, but life sometimes gives no choice and as a consequence Irini and I, from quite separate events and circumstances, are alone in this world.' Anna closes her mouth and looks at the floor. She has finished her speech.

The air is still now, the dust suspended, undisturbed. No one moves, or coughs, or twitches. The moment feels unbreakable.

'I had no blood family for thirty-five years,' Petta exhales loudly. 'I don't care who has done what. For me, this is about moving forward.' The air swirls with his energy.

'Eleni...' Marina offers. 'I love you.' Her tone of voice whispers a thousand sorries, her heart on a plate, an absorption of blame. There is a momentary pause. Someone coughs and the spell is broken.

Eleni steps towards Marina. Marina hungrily pulls Eleni to her and encloses her in her arms. Petta cannot resist, and he wraps his longs arms around them both. Irini claps her hands together once and then interlocks her fingers to stop herself doing it again. Panos steps back into the room and puts an arm around Irini and gives her a supportive squeeze.

'What! The moment my back is turned you find a girlfriend?' It is Panos's boyfriend. Petta releases Eleni and Marina, and all of them are smiling.

Later that evening, at Zoe's, Marina is pressed for every detail. Bobby has a smug look on his face, aware of the part he played in the turn of events.

'So you tracked down every one of the boys in Petta's class and one by one ruled them out?' Zoe is crying with laughter. 'I have never heard anything so absurd.'

'I thought it was pretty smart!' Bobby says. He is in the shadows, which are being kind to him, reflecting his younger self.

'You would, you cunning old fox. But well done, Marina. Families are tricky things. It sounds like you handled it well, if bizarrely.'

The door opens with a bang and Irini rushes in, out of breath. 'We are getting married!' The sun streams in behind her and Marina blinks at the sudden light.

'Yes, we know, Irini.' Zoe lifts a spoon to her mother's lips.

'No, I mean immediately, the day after tomorrow. Petta says he will wait no more, life's too short and all that. He's talked to Socrates.' She turns to Marina. 'The papas. Remember, Marina? You met him in the hospital.'

'Can I be a bridesmaid?' Roula is watching a western. She is standing, her arms dangling by her sides, and she has drawn her fingers at the ready for a shoot-out.

'We were just going to have a quiet little wedding.'

'And then a huge party!' Bobby says.

'Why not?' Zoe agrees.

'No money,' Irini answers.

'You don't need money. We are all family here on the island. If everyone brings a little something we'll be fine.'

The taxi boat men do not want Petta to have a low-key wedding. They agree he should get married in style. But they do not arrange this with Petta or Irini. Petta's parents, Mr and Mrs Mavromati on the farm, are approached and Marina is invited to their house for the discussion.

They are an elderly couple, more like grandparents. Marina is touched by their warmth towards her. They repeatedly say how her sadness in losing Petta became their joy and how much they love him, in a tone to reassure Marina that they have been good loving parents to him. His mother impresses upon Marina how she never let Petta think they were his birth parents and she always made sure he had his butterfly hanky with him. 'Like an anchor,' she says. 'But,' she adds with a sigh, 'we are poor and the farm is not ours. The lease will end when we die. It will make me so happy to see him married, something we could not help him with…' There are tears in the old lady's eyes.

Marina is surprised at how little they need to say to each other to make the situation comfortable. Which is just as well, as the taxi boat men have a lot to say, mostly loudly, with arms flying in gesticulation. Eventually Mrs Mavromati brings out Greek coffee and ouzo chasers and the discussion becomes even louder. Mr Mavromati is enjoying the noise and joins in with the shouting as much as he can. Finally, when the coffees and ouzos have all been drunk, the taxi boat men come to an agreement and everyone is sworn to secrecy. One man volunteers to tell Socrates, the papas, but another says he will do it and there is a secondary raising of voices in which everyone is assigned a role. Those who are given bureaucratic roles grumble a little, and Mrs Mavromati pours them each a second ouzo.

There are surprises for everyone. Marina calls Juliet and invites her over. Juliet is thrilled. Eleni calls her sister, Artemis, in Athens, and she and her new husband Sotos make arrangements to arrive the next day. Panos calls all his and Petta's classmates and every one of them, including sour-faced Yanni, is delighted.

Marina tells Zoe the secret plan for the wedding and Zoe says that, obviously, she cannot come with her family, which disappoints Marina, but she can see why. Bobby is listening.

'And the party afterwards, where will that be held?'

'Oh, no one has discussed that.'

'Have it here then, in the square, with tables and chairs from Irini and Petta's house, and from the rented rooms. Then at least I can come,' Bobby says. Aunt Eleftheria wakes up at his jiggling happiness shaking through the chairs.

The day of the wedding arrives before everything has been arranged. Petta stays the night on his parents' farm. Marina stays with Irini.

The taxi boat men go to pick up Petta, and as he marches to the church they manoeuvre him in a different direction.

'Hey, guys, come on! I'll be late.' But they are not to be deterred. They take him down to the port where several guests have already arrived.

Marina helps Irini dress. She has been lent the most beautiful white lace dress by Zoe's mum. It was her wedding dress. Panos arrives to stand in for Irini's father, and he leads her out to the street where Yanni waits, twisting his moustache, dressed in a suit and looking distinctly uncomfortable, his donkey beautifully adorned with ribbons and flowers. Panos lifts little Irini on, side-saddle, and they set off for the church, only to turn down towards the port. Yanni tells Irini to trust him, as he twists his handlebars.

By the time Irini gets to the port, Petta and the guests are nowhere to be seen. There is a yacht in port, which is covered with pale orange bougainvillea, wound into the stays and along the boom, and littered over the deck. Irini is helped aboard. Costas Voulgaris, the millionaire waiter, wishes her welcome. Marina climbs on board, followed by Panos.

The yacht has a different movement from the water taxi, a slower, more even roll. But the water is like oil and there is not a breath of air. The engine ticks over, driving them effortlessly from the harbour.

Out in the channel they turn west towards the end of the island where Ship Rock lies. Irini is grinning and chattering and cannot sit still. Panos is fussing with her hair. Marina sits and takes it all in. The view down the channel still lifts her like no other. She feels proud of her family.

'So, where are we going?' Irini is looking up and down the coast for clues. Panos makes one last tweak to her hair and sets her free. She can still see no trace of anything on shore and they are fast coming up to the boatyard.

The millionaire waiter-come-captain turns the yacht hard to starboard and they swing round to face out to sea.

Irini gasps. A dozen taxi boats are circling the tiny island with the church. One taxi is moored to the quay. The yacht lowers its anchor, its keel too deep to allow it to moor close to the island. A taxi boat comes to carry Marina, Irini and Panos to shore.

The island is even smaller than it looked from the sea. Petta and his parents take all the room there is by the church door. The church inside is so small that only the papas, the couple and the best man can fit. Two large decorated candles provide some light.

Panos walks Irini up the quay and hands her to Petta, and then swaps sides to become the best man. The papas begins his incantations. He changes from quiet Socrates Rappas into a bellowing priest. Marina, peering in through the church doorway, takes out her hanky to dry her eyes. The rings are exchanged, and the couple are crowned three times by the papas and then three times by Panos. They can hear cheers from the boats, which have all stopped circling and are crowding as close as they can to the island.

The couple sip from the wine chalice, and then Socrates the papas asks who will be the stronger of the two. Marina cringes as she remembers this part of her own wedding. The stamping of the toes. Whoever stamps on the other's toes first will be the boss. Her toes were bruised.

Irini makes to stamp on Petta's toes, but he is too quick. He lifts her in the air and lowers both her feet upon his toes and whispers, 'I wouldn't have it any other way.' Marina can feel herself blushing and turns away as if she is intruding on a private moment. But the boats all around sound their horns and Marina laughs. The taxi boat men compete to sound their horns the longest, recent memories of the pirate re-enactment igniting their endeavours. Costas Voulgaris sets off a flare on his yacht, which starts a trend. The port police have come in uniform on the port police boat. One of the crew, who is smoking a cigarette, fires a gun repeatedly in the air. The noise echoes off the island and people instinctively duck.

Eleni is leaning on the prow of one of the larger boats taking photographs with a long-lens camera. Marina smiles and waves; Eleni waves back, still pointing her camera at the island.

Petta and Irini make their way to the yacht and they are left to sail back to the island alone.

Marina and Panos join Eleni. The papas nearly falls in the water as he climbs aboard the port police boat. The police cheer when he saves himself.

Costas Voulgaris surprises them all. When they return to the square he has all but transferred his whole café there. The tables match and are covered with white tablecloths. There are waiters, albeit in jeans, but they have white shirts on. There is a jug of wine on every table and people are bringing plates of steaming food out from crates, strapped to donkeys, that have come up from his kitchens.

Zoe is sitting at a table with her mum, Bobby, Roula and a sleeping Aunt Eleftheria. With a trembling hand, Bobby is drinking Aunt Eleftheria's wine, his own glass already empty. Maria the candlemaker is sitting with them, her phone on the table.

To Marina's utmost joy, she sees that Artemis and her husband are here. They say they arrived by the first ferry, in time to see the wedding. Eleni explained it all over the phone and they think it is fantastic. Artemis says she cannot wait to get to know Petta better, and could they all celebrate next Easter at the village? They agree it's a date.

Soon everyone is dancing. They dance the *syrtaki* in a line, arm over arm, snaking around the tables, followed by the complex foot-sliding *hassapiko*. As they get their breath back, a boy of no more than ten dances the slow-strutting *zeybekiko*. With people half kneeling and clapping to encourage him, he dances like a drunk. On and on they dance. The music changes to a series of harsh, raw Cretan war dances, and the men are up and stamping their feet, dancing the *pentozali*. Marina is mesmerised and wishes she was not so stout.

She slowly backs away from the hub of the party and sits on the bench by the peeling grey door, watching everyone enjoying themselves. It is a perfect moment. Irini looks wonderful in her lace gown. She comes over and sits by Marina's side.

'How perfect is this!' Marina says.

'Marina, I want you to be the first to know, I am pregnant....' Irini jumps up from the bench and is dancing with Yanni before Marina has time to reply.

Tears flow as she laughs. Life could not be more perfect.

Marina looks up through the throng of dancers and, for a moment, there in the middle, she sees Meli, dancing and laughing, his lithe body full of rhythm, life, the same sparkle in his eyes as that night so long ago. And then he is gone, hidden in the crowd. She searches for him amongst the dancers, her heart yearning for a second glimpse; she begins to stand to be ready to run to him as soon as he reappears. But, as quickly as her love has grown to full strength again, she knows that, of course, this is not – could not be – Meli. He was lost to her years ago. Her throat constricts, tears fill her eyes, she lowers her weight back onto the bench. She has seen Petta dancing and mistaken him for his father. What is Meli doing now, she wonders, and does he think of her? She has rarely allowed herself to think of him over the years; the pain is too much to bear. Life, she reasons, gives moments of joy, and snatches them away, replacing them with years of sorrow. Better not to dwell on these things.

Tonight is one of those moments. Joyful, bursting with love and perfection. Tomorrow – who knows what tomorrow will bring? But for tonight, whatever sorrow might follow, all she can do is dance.

Petta is winding his way through the crowd towards her, laughing. He takes her hand and pulls her to her feet; he wipes away her tears with his thumb, kisses her on her forehead and swings her in a dance across the flags.

'Lady,' he says breathlessly. 'I told you you would dance with me at my wedding!'

Marina seizes the moment and dances.

If you enjoyed *Black Butterflies* please share it with a friend, and check out the other books in the Greek Village Series!

I'm always delighted to receive email from readers, and I welcome new friends on Facebook.

https://www.facebook.com/authorsaraalexi
saraalexi@me.com

Happy reading,

Sara Alexi

Printed in Great Britain
by Amazon